Codas
and
Calibers

Dan DeKoning

DEDICATION

This book is dedicated to everyone who enjoys reading a good mystery.

And to all the writers who create them.

Codas
and
Calibers

CHAPTER ONE

I didn't think I could eat another piece of cherry pie, and to be honest, cherry pie isn't even my favorite type of pie, but I couldn't say no to Tammy. I don't think anyone in history ever said no to Tammy. She was too strong of a personality for that. But, instead of pushing myself away from the table like a sane person, I insisted on finishing the last of my lemonade. In the space of those twenty seconds, another slice appeared in front of me like the results of a magic trick.

"And that's when I caught her in the barn with the prom queen." Granny Tammy slammed a hand on the table hard enough to make the plates jump and started to laugh so heartily that she eventually broke into a coughing fit.

I glanced over at Laurel to see how she was handling the conversation, and although she was smiling, I noticed that not only was the grin fake, but she forced it as well. Her eyes darted around the room as if she was looking for a piece of furniture to hide behind.

To not seem rude, I ate a fork full of pie and smiled as I did so. Bozeman enjoyed the story, though, since his belly laugh seemed genuine.

I didn't remember if Laurel said her grandmother was in her early seventies or early eighties, but she looked decades younger than that. In fact, Granny Tammy had the same long red hair that topped Laurel's head. If it weren't for the silver streak of hair running right down the middle, someone might have mistaken them for sisters. Besides her youthful appearance, Granny Tammy was young, almost a teenager at heart. She loved to tell stories and jokes, and unprompted, would occasionally break into song.

"Is that story true, Laurel?" Bozeman asked.

If I were sitting within reach, I would have kicked him in the shin under the table to save Laurel from further embarrassment. But because I'm a couple inches short of five feet, my little legs wouldn't reach him. Unless I slid way down in my chair, which would certainly take the discretion away.

Laurel's attention turned to Bozeman for the briefest of moments before she looked Granny Tammy in the eyes. "Not entirely. Janie was the homecoming queen. Not the prom queen."

Everyone was silent for a moment. Surprisingly, it was Laurel who broke into the first bout of laughter, and the others followed suit.

I ate another bite of the pie, sighed, and pushed the plate away, not far, only enough to trigger the idea that I really didn't want or need any more.

Granny Tammy spotted the motion with her sharp eyes. "Don't you like the pie?"

I dabbed at my mouth with a napkin. "Oh, no, I love the pie. I'm so full I can't eat anymore."

Granny Tammy frowned. "You should really eat it. Codi, you look much too thin. You can't weigh more than a hundred pounds."

Bozeman finished his slice, and pushed his plate away, too. "She only breaks a hundred when she's wearing her heavy cowboy boots."

I shot a glare at Bozeman, the one I always did when I wasn't happy with him. "Thanks, Boze. Can I take the pie with me and finish it later?"

Without a word, Granny Tammy turned and walked to a cabinet next to the stove. When she opened the door, I could see there were dozens of different sized plastic containers in there. She rummaged around until she selected one, found a matching cover, and handed it to me. I took the container, which, based on the size and shape previously held sliced ham, and transferred my pie from the plate to the container. After I licked a bit of cherry filling from my finger, I snapped the red cover on top.

"Thanks, I appreciate it," I said.

"I'd give you the rest of the pie, but Maura Sanders is coming over later for tea, and I want to save her some. You don't have to return that. You wash that out and save it when you're finished with the pie. There's always a need for a good plastic container."

I nodded, and to an extent, I agreed. I've got plenty of them myself, holding everything from cat treats to guitar picks. Bozeman has one filled with random nuts, bolts, screws, and nails that appear from nowhere, and we don't know what they belong to. Of course, the little containers can be overkill. When you have so many in the fridge that you need to open a dozen of them before you find what you're looking for, you've gone too far.

"So, how did you meet?" Granny Tammy asked.

I glanced at Laurel, who looked at me, expecting I should answer.

"We were both on the same bill, going to play at the same concert," I explained.

"You were in the band with that Timmy singer, right dear?"

Since Granny Tammy had addressed Laurel directly, she fielded the question. "Toby, Granny. Toby Madden. He had… an accident, and the band disbanded. Codi and Bozeman were nice enough to take me on."

The simple statement impressed me. Laurel summarized nicely how at our last gig Toby Madden got murdered and Bozeman ended up accused of the crime. In the end, though, everything worked out okay.

"That was nice of them," Granny Tammy said.

"It was no problem, actually," I said. "We've been wanting to add a fiddle player to the band, so we're lucky to have her. Laurel's very talented."

Granny Tammy reached out for my hand, and when I offered it, she practically pulled me from the chair. "Come with me."

I followed her through the house to the front stairs and up the creaking steps to a bedroom at the back of the house. For the most part, it looked like any other guest bedroom I've ever seen. There was a twin bed positioned on the far wall, nestled between two windows, perfectly made with a dark blue comforter and pink throw pillows on top. In the corner sat a dresser topped with a vase of fake flowers. For a moment, I couldn't understand why Granny Tammy had brought me up here until she pointed to the largest wall. I stepped to the middle of the wall and gazed at the dozens of photographs, awards, and accolades of Laurel.

There were several closeups of her playing in a symphony, dressed to the nines in a tuxedo, and several of her standing alone, center stage, working the bow. Another shot caught my eye. Laurel with her foot on a hay bale, wearing overalls with one strap undone, a straw cowgirl hat on her head. She wore a smile on her face far more prominent than in any other photo on the wall. Then there were the awards, running from junior high school through college. Disbursed among them were several newspaper articles with grainy black-and-white photos of Laurel. I turned to ask Granny Tammy a question, but she had disappeared.

I retraced my steps back to the kitchen and found Granny Tammy back in her seat. When Laurel saw me, she rolled her eyes and looked like she wanted to turn into water and slip through the floorboards. "Oh no, she showed it to you, didn't she?"

I grinned. "Yep, she sure did."

"Showed her what?" Bozeman asked.

"Why, I call it Laurel's Wall of Fame," Granny Tammy answered.

Laurel rolled her eyes again. "More like a Wall of Shame," she muttered, just audibly.

"There's nothing to be ashamed of," I said. "It's amazing. I wish my parents had something like that. Granny Tammy, how did you feel when Laurel turned from being a classical violinist to being a fiddle player in a country band?"

Granny Sammy's head dropped. "I have to admit, I was a little disappointed."

Silence engulfed the room. After a beat, Granny Tammy raised her head, her gray eyes glinting. "Disappointed that I couldn't join her on the road and go to every concert."

Bozeman and I laughed, and Laurel finally cracked a smile.

"Well, there's plenty of room on the bus. You could always be our roadie," I offered.

Granny Tammy shook her head. "No, dear, that's quite all right. I'm too old now to go traipsing all over the country. Besides, I have a weekly bridge game that I host, and I volunteer at the community center, and there are a couple of ladies I take to appointments and for groceries."

"You're right, you're much too important here to come along with us," Laurel said.

"That doesn't mean I don't want to hear about your adventures, of course."

Laurel got to her feet and gave Granny Tammy a hug. "I promise to write you a letter every week."

Granny Tammy returned the hug and scoffed. "I don't want

a letter. Text me or send me a video! I'm not old, you know."

Laurel gave Granny Tammy a kiss on the forehead and went to the sink to attend to the dishes. "Hey, one of you two come on over here. I'll wash, and you dry."

Bozeman rocked back in his chair for a second and got up and joined Laurel at the sink. He picked up a towel and stood ready to receive dishes.

Granny Tammy settled back in her chair. "Laurel hasn't told me much about you."

I could understand that. Laurel had only been with us for a little over a week, and we'd known her only a skosh longer than that.

"There's not much to tell. Bozeman and I travel the music circuit from the great plains to the Pacific Ocean, playing music and living life."

Granny Tammy turned in her chair and watched Bozeman for a moment. He stood over six feet, was under two hundred pounds, and had abs you could play xylophone on. He looked absolutely ridiculous crammed next to the sink, trying to dry a teacup with his large, athletic hands. "Is he your fella?"

I smiled. "No way. He's not really my type. We're merely business partners. He drives the bus, plays guitar, provides backup vocals. Partners."

"You live on that big bus? Only the two of you, traveling the country and you're only partners?"

"Yep. I assure you, there's nothing going on. You want a tour of the bus?"

Granny Tammy's eyes brightened. "I thought you'd never ask!"

Granny Tammy was on her feet and halfway to the back door before I was even out of my chair. When I caught up to her, she was standing by the side of the bus, staring at the writing on the side.

"Well, look at that. Codi Cassidy. Your name's on the bus."

"Yes, ma'am. That way, I know which one is mine. Come on aboard."

I opened the door and held it while Granny Tammy climbed the steps, and I joined her in the living room and kitchen area. "Sorry, it's a little messy right now."

The kitchen was in its typically tidy order, but the dinette held Laurel's few bags and violin cases.

"Is this where Laurel sleeps?" Granny Tammy asked.

I was a little embarrassed, especially since the grand tour would show off the other areas of the bus, including the private rooms Bozeman and I both had.

"It's temporary. She's only been with us a week, and it will take a little time to get her settled. Don't worry, though, that dinette converts to a nice comfy bed. Come on, I'll show you the rest."

Granny Tammy followed me down a short corridor, and just past the kitchen, I opened the first door I came to. "This is Bozeman's room."

She stepped in and looked around. Bozeman was a neat freak. He made his bed with hospital corners. On his small desk was a mug filled with a half dozen pens, and next to that was a spiral notebook, laid open to the page of the latest song he was writing. Nothing was out of place, all his clothing and belongings tucked away into drawers, cabinets, and crannies. Granny Tammy nodded and followed me to the next door.

"This is our storage room. This is where we keep our equipment. The first chance we get, we're going to reconfigure this and turn it into Laurel's room."

Granny Tammy stepped into the space and found herself surrounded by totes of cables, guitar cases, amplifiers, and microphone stands. "Will she have room in here?"

"Oh yes. It was originally a bedroom, but since there were only two of us, we converted it to storage. It'll be easy enough to change it right back. Come on, I'll show you my room."

The next room was the small bathroom, just large enough for a toilet, small vanity, and a shower half the size of an old-fashioned phone booth.

My room was next. The door was halfway open, so Granny Tammy pushed it open and stepped in. Unlike Bozeman, I'm not a neat freak. I made my bed, but not neatly. There was a T-shirt on the bed, the one I'd slept in the night before. My small desk had the same Codi Cassidy branded coffee mug that Bozeman had. Instead of pens, I filled mine with hair ties, guitar picks, spare change, buttons, and anything else I picked up that fit in the mug. Instead of one notebook, my desk held my laptop, which was perched on top of three notebooks, and on top of the computer was a paperback that I was working my way through. The closet door was partially open, and there was one lone cowgirl boot on the floor at the foot of the bed.

"Oh, my lord," Granny Tammy exclaimed as she put her hands on her cheeks.

I thought she was freaking out about the mess, but then she made a beeline for the bed and reached for my tuxedo.

Gibson, my cat, saw her coming. As usual, he was napping atop a pile of pillows on the bed. He looked at her with one tired eye, then opened both wide when she swept him up, sat on the bed, put him on her lap, and started petting him.

"What's his name?"

"Gibson. I named him after my favorite guitar."

She leaned over as she petted him, and started speaking to him like he was a toddler. "Who's a good boy? Who's a wuzza, wuzza, wuzza?"

I wasn't quite sure what a wuzza was, but Gibson seemed to know and started purring loudly enough for me to hear him from where I stood by the door. I watched for a few minutes as she nuzzled with the cat. Then she stood and placed Gibson back where she'd found him. Gibson stretched out one back leg, then the other, then did a couple of slow circles and settled back to his nap like nothing had happened.

"I just love animals," Granny Tammy said as we headed back to the bus door. "Did I mention as a little girl I lived on a farm in Missouri?"

I shook my head. "No, you didn't."

"We had every animal imaginable. Cows, of course. Horses, goats, pigs, chickens, ducks. I even had a pet turtle. A turtle! Have you ever heard of having such a creature as a pet?"

I smiled, then motioned for her to follow me. We stepped off the bus, and I went to one of the storage compartments, crouched over, and invited Granny Tammy to do the same.

"Take a gander in here."

I moved over, and Granny Tammy filled my space. Beyond a makeshift chicken wire door were two creatures, each sleeping on their own blanket.

"Is that a raccoon?"

I nodded. "Yep. That's Dolly, the world-famous three-legged raccoon."

Out of habit, I opened the door and ran my hand under her blanket. I found a marble, removed my hand, and closed the door. I held up the marble for Granny Tammy to see, then dropped it into her palm.

"She's always collecting trinkets on her nightly adventures. If I didn't confiscate them, her little home would be full of junk in a month."

Granny Tammy stared at the marble. A perfect cat's eye. "What do you do with it all?"

"It depends. If it belongs in nature, like sticks, rocks, leaves, stuff like that, I send it back to nature. Trash goes in the trash, coins go into the pet food budget bucket, and some things I keep for her. I've got half a gallon-sized ice cream bucket filled with things she's collected. Now and then, I open the bucket for her, and she likes to rummage through it and rediscover things. She's almost like a kid cleaning out the toy box and finding things to play with that they forgot they had."

Granny Tammy nodded. She handed me back the marble, and I shoved it in my pocket. She looked into the cage at Dolly's roommate. "Is that a cat? It looks like Gibson."

"Nope. That is Merle. He's a skunk."

Granny Tammy took a tentative step back, but since she was crouched over, she almost fell on her butt. I reached out and steadied her.

"Don't worry. He's de-scented, playful, and extremely friendly."

"How in the world did you get a raccoon and a skunk?"

I got up, then started walking to the rear of the bus. "Those two I rescued from a vet. Neither one would make it out in the wild, and he couldn't find a home for them, so they came to live with me. Then there's these two guys."

In the back of the bus was a brick-sized hole, and behind the chicken wire were two chipmunks. They were in the middle of running circles around each other, and when they saw me, they stopped and came to the cage front.

"This is Willie and Waylon." I dipped my hand into my pocket and pulled out four whole peanuts. I passed them through the wire, and Willie and Waylon gathered them up and took them further into their domain. "They just showed up one day and made a nest in this rusted-out hole. I cleaned it up a little, and made them a home, too."

Granny Tammy passed me a stern, unhappy look. "Are they happy living on a bus, caged up like this?"

"Oh, no. It's not usually like this. When we're in a location for more than a few hours, they get a full run of the world. Willie and Waylon usually go out during the day, climb trees, look for food, run around and do whatever they do to occupy their time. Dolly and Merle are mostly nocturnal and prefer to wander around at night. Then, like magic, they all come back to the bus."

"That doesn't sound too bad, I guess."

"Of course not. They have all the freedom they want. More than we humans, sometimes."

"But you won't let them out tonight?"

"Nope. Not until tomorrow when we get to our next gig in Monterey."

CHAPTER TWO

I must admit that the road trip from Bakersfield to Monterey isn't one of my favorites. I'm more of a mountain view girl, and the trip up I-5 presents nothing but rolling hills and farmland. Fortunately for me, I now have Laurel as a traveling companion, because when Bozeman is driving, he's not much on conversation. Every hundred miles or so he'll say something, but it's always something uninspiring like 'there's a rest stop coming up', or 'I'm going to stop soon for gas'. On past adventures, I'd have to spend my time napping or reading, and although I love Gibson with all my heart, he's not a skilled conversationalist.

Instead of watching the mile markers pass by, Laurel and I were hard at work on the set list for tomorrow's gig.

Working from an email I received, I read off the list of special requests and Laurel jotted them down on a sheet of paper.

"*Celebration*? The Kool & The Gang song? Seriously?" she said.

I smiled. "Yep, that's the one. It would amaze you some of the strange requests we get when people book a gig. Granted, we'll usually throw in a few, and sometimes a lot of the songs are ones we rotate in and out of the set list anyway, but a lot of times people will send in requests that are either too ambitious or too outrageous for the two of us to handle. Let me see that."

Laurel moved the paper so I could see it more clearly. I took a pen from the table and crossed a line through *Celebration* and three other songs, circled three others, and put dots next to the remaining four.

"What's the shorthand mean?" Laurel asked.

"The crossed off ones are hard passes. Either we don't know them, or we'd never play them. Circles mean that they're already on the set list. Dots mean they're in limbo at this point, neither in nor out. Bozeman and I, and now you, usually decide together which of those we'd include."

"You don't simply put them in?"

I shook my head. "Not usually. The way we typically set up the list is a few of my original songs, a few of Bozeman's original songs, and then the rest we fill with covers."

"How long is a typical show?"

"Between an hour and ninety minutes. Sometimes longer. We got booked for a wedding once and played for almost three and a half hours. I love to perform, but even for me that was stretching it, especially for a two-person band."

"Okay, so what's next?" Laurel asked.

I got up and retrieved a bottle of water for myself and one for Laurel and returned to the dinette.

"Now we get to the fun part. We use computerized backing tracks to provide a more full-band sound, including bass, drums, and, of course, fiddle. We need to figure out where to remove the fiddle parts so you can take their place."

Laurel uncapped the bottle and took a drink of water. Some dribbled out onto her chin, but she wiped it away with a nonchalance that made me think it happened all the time.

"It sounds hard," she said.

I shook my head. "Sounds worse than it actually is. All I

need to do is go into the sound file of the song and uncheck the box that says 'fiddle'."

"That sounds easy," Laurel admitted.

"Here's the plan. We'll go through all the songs we have in our library, see if they have a fiddle in them, and see if you can play the song. If you can't, we'll either remove it from the list if it's a cover, or we'll take a note if it's an original, so you can learn it."

Laurel agreed, so I pulled my laptop from the seat next to me, put it on the table, and brought up my music library.

We'd gotten about halfway through the list when I sensed the bus decelerate. I looked out the window and saw that we were pulling into a rest area. Before long, the bus shifted into Park between two semi-trucks that were also headed northbound.

"Let's go," I said as I stood. "The general rule is, one goes, all goes. Bozeman hates cleaning out the bus toilet, so we make use of public facilities whenever we can. Besides, it's good to stretch the legs."

Bozeman waited while Laurel and I got off the bus and followed behind and locked the doors. He stretched his arms in the air, touched his toes a couple of times and headed off for the men's room without a word.

"He doesn't talk much, does he?" Laurel asked as we followed the sidewalk to the toilets.

"Not really. Sometimes he gets on a roll and will talk your ears off, but generally, he's pretty quiet. You were thinking maybe it was you?"

I glanced over at Laurel, and she nodded. "Well, don't worry about it. Quiet is his nature. If he has something to say, he'll say it, and he'll always answer questions when you ask them."

Laurel nodded again. Then we finished our walk and parted ways when we moved to separate stalls. Five minutes later, I was back outside in the sunshine. I found a bench, sat down, closed my eyes, and lifted my face to the sun. I heard it said that it's bad for my skin to do that, but at the moment, I didn't care since I loved the warmth on my face and the quiet moment I had for myself.

"Hey, little lady, you need a ride?"

The voice shattered my silence, so I opened my eyes and looked at the road warrior who was speaking to me. Overalls hid a body that was at least double the weight it should have been, and a greased-stained trucker hat covered a head of hair that hadn't seen a barber in months. He clearly needed a bath, since he smelled like a mix of corn chips and hot dogs.

"No thanks. I have my own ride."

He stepped closer. "Come on, baby. I know you want me."

I wondered if the guy was a card-carrying member of the sleaze-of-the-month club based on that awful line. But I figured it was time to leave, which wasn't a problem because I had my own keys to the bus. The only thing I worried about was if the jerk was idiotic enough to follow me.

I got up from the bench and took a few steps toward the parking lot. Behind me, I heard him grunt, and I could tell by the shifting shadow on the sidewalk that he did indeed intend to follow me.

"Hey." He grabbed my shoulder, trying to spin me around.

That was all the encouragement I needed. Many people, when they deal with me, assume that I'm not powerful. That bad assumption is because I'm short and skinny. I swung around, and as I did, I performed a perfect uppercut that connected square on with the trucker's private parts. That took the fight and bravado right out of him, and both of his hands went right to his groin before he groaned and dropped to his knees. I took two steps back to make sure his gumption was truly gone. I was about to turn back around and head to the bus when I spotted a small crowd of people watching the entire encounter. Laurel and

Bozeman among them.

A few seconds later, Bozeman appeared at my side. "You need any help here?" He looked down at the trucker, who at that moment rolled over from his knees onto his side.

I smiled and locked arms with him. "Oh, my hero! No. I think I'll be okay." We waited for Laurel to catch up to us and climbed back on the bus.

"Does that sort of thing happen a lot?" Laurel asked as we settled back into our seats.

"Not as much as it used to. Early in our touring career, we played a lot of bars and honkytonks. I'm sure you know the places. Long wood bar, sawdust on the floor, chicken wire in front of the stage. It got to where if I didn't have drunken cowboys attempt to pick me up at least three times over the course of the night, I started feeling bad about myself."

"So, what happened?"

"I decided to stop playing shows in those places. Now we do mostly private events, theme parks, festivals, county fairs, places like that. Bar gigs are rare for us now, but occasionally we'll pick one up."

"Sounds nice. See this?"

Laurel turned to her left and pointed to her right arm, an inch above the elbow. I moved in close and saw a half-inch scar she was pointing to.

"Let me guess, flying beer bottle shard?" I asked.

"How did you guess that?" Laurel said as she rubbed the spot.

I smiled, stood, and turned around. I pushed down the back of my jeans a couple of inches and pointed to my own scar. "Because I have one exactly like it."

Laurel grinned. "We're twins."

I laughed with her and retook my seat. "Come on, let's finish going through the songs."

Laurel and I hunkered down and concentrated on the task

while Bozeman kept us rolling down the road. The timing was good because we finished our task and I had just shut down the laptop when Bozeman pulled into the parking lot of a diner. I looked out the window and saw the four lanes of California Highway 1, and beyond that, sand that led into the waters of Monterey Bay.

"Is this the place?" I asked as Bozeman appeared from the front. "It's a lot less fancy than I would have figured."

Bozeman smiled at me. "It's not the place. It's where—"

A knock at the door interrupted Bozeman, and since he was the one closest to it, he opened it. I heard him express his greetings, then he stepped backward to let someone else aboard. The black man who stepped onto the bus was large enough to make the bus sway as he climbed the stairs. I guessed he was at least three times my weight, and from what I could tell, he was all muscle. Dark blue jeans obscured his legs, but based on the arms and torso definition beneath his T-shirt, I guessed he had a lot lower body fat percentage than I did. I think I could have played xylophone on his abs. Seeing the man would have been intimidating under different circumstances. However, the enormous smile on his face and the way he swept Bozeman into his giant arms for a bear hug told me all I needed to know about the man.

"This is my old friend, Loren Mullen," Bozeman said, once he escaped the clutches of his buddy. "Loren, this is Codi Cassidy, and Laurel Preston."

Loren greeted us both with a hug, and I literally felt like a letter being stuffed into an envelope when he grabbed me.

"I'm honored to meet you both," he said, the smile never leaving his face.

"You look like you lost weight, Loren. Have you been feeling okay?" Bozeman asked.

"Oh, come on now, Boze. Don't tease me like that. You know it ain't right."

"Want to sit down?" I asked.

"No ma'am, I'm fine standing, and we'll only be here for but a minute."

I was grateful for the answer since I honestly didn't know if we had a piece of furniture on board that would hold him.

"Where are we going?" Laurel asked.

The grin reappeared on Loren's face. "For pie, of course."

The way he said it made me think that going for pie was the only logical answer, but I was always up for pie, so I didn't mind. Even though I still had a slice in the fridge to work through.

"If y'all are ready, you can follow me."

Whether we were ready or not, Loren backtracked to the stairs and stepped back off the bus, rocking the boat as he did. Bozeman, who was ready, followed him right off. Laurel and I both took a minute to slip on our shoes, and Laurel grabbed a light jacket from the chair.

Loren crossed the parking lot with his long legs in what seemed like six strides, while I had to do triple-steps to keep up with him. To his credit, he waited at the door and held it open for the rest of us. Once inside, he guided us to the back corner to the largest booth in the place. The booth was in a shape of a U, and although two sides were the standard booths found in thousands of diners across the country. The third side was a wood pew that looked like someone had liberated from a church.

Loren took his place in the center of the pew, and the rest of us slid into the booths.

"You have your own seat at the table?" Bozeman asked.

Loren lifted an arm and waved his hand in the air.

"Seat at the table? I own this place."

Bozeman shook his head. "No way. Sign out front says Lulu's."

Loren grinned. "Yes, it's mine. I had to do something with my time and my money after my playing days were over. And Lulu is my mom. I named the place after her. After all, it's her recipes I use for the pies."

As if on cue, two servers appeared. One was carrying plates and silverware, the other had a large tray with a variety of pie slices on it. Once they spread the pies across the table, the server took drink orders, then disappeared.

"Dig in. There's apple, cherry, French silk, pecan, peach, mixed berry, and Key lime. Or, if there's something else you'd rather have, just say the word and I can make it happen."

I didn't want to offend Loren, so I reached out for the slice of French silk and at the same time Laurel went for the Key lime. I grabbed a spoon and dug in. The chocolate goodness exploded my taste buds. I thought for a moment that I'd die happy right then, and based on the moan coming from Laurel, the lime was just as wonderful.

"This is amazing," I said between bites.

Loren leaned back and grinned. "Thank you. I'll tell mama you liked them."

Bozeman had polished off a slice of apple before I'd even made it partway through my slice, then pointed his fork at Loren. "You sell a lot of these? You must."

Loren grinned even wider than he had before. "Enough to keep this entire business afloat. Besides the pies I sell here, I get special orders like mad. I have three delivery people on staff that do nothing but drive around all day transporting pies. I cover all over the region, including up to San Francisco."

"That many pies? Every day?" Laurel asked.

"Yep," Loren said with a look of pride on his face.

"Why go through the trouble of having a diner instead of just a bakery?" Bozeman asked.

"I make the pies off-site. The diner I keep open to please the locals and the travelers who whiz on by at fifty miles an hour. It also helps keep a bunch of people in town employed. I couldn't close down the diner. These folks are my family, not just my employees."

Laurel giggled and rolled her eyes. "Isn't that what the boss always says?"

"Usually, but in this case, it's true. Everyone makes more than a living wage and has a full benefits package, including health care and paid time off. There's even a retirement plan match I do."

Bozeman grinned in between bites, which made him look silly considering there was a small pecan attached to his chin. "I don't even have one of those. Can I have a job here?"

It was Loren's turn to grin, and he grinned widely, his white teeth looking like two rows of perfectly set tombstones.

"Sorry, man, I'm actually over-staffed at the moment. Besides, knowing you, you'd get bored out of your skull by the end of the first day."

Bozeman shrugged, licked his fork clean, and pushed the plate aside. He didn't say another word, just leaned back in his chair and folded his arms over his chest, looking satisfied, like a cat just finishing a hearty meal.

Although I wanted to keep going, I didn't want to embarrass myself by opening the top button on my jeans. I pushed my plate aside as well without bothering to lick the fork clean, even though I wanted to.

"Bozeman tells me we've got you to thank for the gig tomorrow," I said. I took a drink of water, set the glass down, and wiped my mouth.

Loren looked at me, and although there was nothing aggressive about his gaze, it seemed like there was something he wanted to say.

"Yeah, that was me. When Mr. Harris' secretary called to order desserts for the party, she let it slip that they were having problems booking entertainment. I knew Bozeman was in the business, so I simply connected the dots."

"You're providing the pie?" Laurel asked.

Loren leaned back in his seat, which creaked under his

mass. "I'm also invited to the party, since I'm considered an upstanding member of the business community."

"Well, we appreciate it. We're always looking for gigs to play." I smiled a genuine smile, and when he saw it, Loren's face drooped a bit. He looked around to see if anyone was listening in, then leaned forward into his booth.

"Did you get paid?" he asked, his voice low.

At first, I didn't understand what he was asking, but then it clicked.

"Forty percent upfront. Our standing booking fee," I said, telling him the truth.

Loren nodded, then moved in even closer, and his voice dropped to just above a whisper. "Listen, I don't want to tell you how to do your business, but make sure you get that other sixty percent before the show starts."

"Why?" I asked.

"This doesn't leave the diner. Hawthorne Harris has a bad habit of forgetting to pay his bills."

"Isn't he like a millionaire?" Bozeman asked.

Loren glanced in Bozeman's direction. "Multi-millionaire is more like it. Unfortunately, he has that annoying problem that some rich people seem to have where he thinks because he's rich, everything should be free for him. And even when people push him to pay, he still tries to cheat them out of what he owes them."

"Then why do you do business with him?" Bozeman asked.

"Like I said, we're part of the same small-town business community. Doesn't look right if I don't play along. Besides, the bakery has a pay-on-order policy, so I always get the money up front. You should take care to do the same."

Loren's attention strayed when an older gentleman approached the booth, took Loren's massive hand in his frail one, and started making small talk.

I looked over at Bozeman. His eyes met mine, and I knew

we were both thinking the same thing.

CHAPTER THREE

"Are you sure we have the right place?" I asked as Bozeman pulled the bus up a driveway and stopped at a gated entry, rolled down his window, and pressed an intercom button.

Bozeman shot me a glance and pointed out the front windshield. I looked and noticed a giant letter H on the iron gate blocking our way.

The intercom let out a squelch of static, then came to life. "Yes? Can I help you?"

Bozeman turned his head to face the voice. "If this is the home of Hawthorne Harris, my name is Bozeman James. I'm here with Codi Cassidy, and we're the entertainment for tonight."

There was a pause and got no response for half a minute and the squelch returned. "Go ahead. Stop at the guard shack."

Before the last syllable cleared the air, the gate clicked and slowly opened inward. Bozeman pulled ahead at a snail's pace. Two hundred yards later, he stopped at the guard shack where a guard dressed like a U.S. Army commando stood in the center of the driveway, blocking the way. As we got closer, he held a hand up in front of him, like he was going to stop the bus with mental powers. The brakes squealed as we came to a halt, and Bozeman stuck his head through the window and said hello. The no-nonsense guard requested to come aboard, so Laurel unlocked the door and let him in.

"Can I see some identification, please?" the guard said without so much as a grunt of greeting.

Bozeman and I got up from the seats in the front and each of us headed off to our respective rooms for our wallets. Since we lived life on the bus, neither of us carried our wallets on our physical person unless we were going somewhere. Like anywhere we needed money or an ID, and even then, I often forgot mine. When I returned with my driver's license, the guard was already scrutinizing Laurel's passport. When he spotted me, I handed him the license, and he took it, compared me against the picture.

"Your hair is different," he said.

He had me there. The photo of me he held in his left hand showed a prematurely graying woman in her mid-thirties. The real-life version of me standing in front of him was sporting a hair color of deep purple, almost raven colored. I hoped it would lighten as a little time passed.

In response to his non-question, I shrugged. "Women, am I right?"

He stared me down, then checked my name off a list on the clipboard he carried and handed the license back to me. By the time he finished that task, Bozeman had appeared and passed over his license. The guard looked at it for half a second, then found an issue with Bozeman's credentials as well.

"The picture's the same, but the name isn't. Your license says your name is Jesse, not Bozeman."

Bozeman gave him his signature grin. "Bozeman's my stage name. I really don't want to be known as Jesse James."

The guard didn't laugh, but checked Bozeman off the sheet and handed the license back. He pointed his pencil in Laurel's direction. "You're not on the list at all."

Laurel opened her mouth to say something, but I held up my hand to stop her and jumped in instead. "Laurel's only been with the band for a couple of weeks. It's my fault. I should have called ahead and let you know she needed to be added to the list, but I didn't do it."

"What does she do?" the grumpy guard asked.

"I play the fiddle," Laurel answered for herself.

The guard looked back at me. I shrugged. "She's right. She plays the fiddle."

The guard turned around and pulled a phone from his pocket. Although he pretended to be discreet, we could all hear him talking to someone about Laurel. After almost five full minutes, he clicked off and put the phone back where it came from.

"Okay, she's good to go." The guard copied her name from the passport to the clipboard, then passed the booklet back to Laurel. "Follow the road down to the left. It'll curve around to the back of the property, and you can park the bus on the basketball court. The caterer's van is already there, so pull in next to that."

Bozeman returned to his place behind the steering wheel, and I got back into the passenger seat. Once we all strapped in, Bozeman put the bus in Drive, waved to the guard, and headed down the driveway. We traveled for a quarter mile before we climbed a hill, and once we crested that, the house finally came into view. House was actually an understatement, because it looked more like a hotel resort than a private residence.

As we descended the hill toward the main building, we saw a private golf course on our right. Beyond that, we saw the edge of an Olympic-sized, in-ground swimming pool. The main building was impressive, especially with the large Doric columns that lined the front entrance. But the view beyond the building, which included a drop into Monterey Bay, and the expanse of the

Pacific Ocean beyond, was unbelievable. By my estimate, there were just under a million different shades of blues and greens underneath the whitecaps that gently lapped their way toward shore. As Bozeman dipped down the hill, we passed three giant oak trees that obscured my view of the ocean enough to snap my thoughts away. Then, before I realized it, Bozeman parked the bus next to a caterer's truck that looked more like a high-end restaurant on wheels than the typical van I was used to seeing. When I stepped off my bus, I noticed a flurry of activity in the caterer's truck. A third of the side opened up, like a food truck. Through the window I saw several people in chef's whites busy at work while several other workers transported goods from the truck into the house.

"You're the band?"

I turned around to look for the owner of the question and saw a man in a dark gray pinstriped suit standing before me with a clipboard.

"Howdy. Yes. We're the band. I'm Codi Cassidy." I stuck out my hand for a shake, and the man inspected it for a moment until he finally accepted it and gave me the shortest shake I'd ever received. He stood straight, shoulders back, heels together. He was six feet tall, wore his light brown hair high and tight.

"I'm Brantley Wilson. I'm Mr. Harris' assistant. Please, follow me." He spun in place without another word, and then, with military precision, walked off toward the main house.

I followed, double-time, in order to keep up with him, and Bozeman and Laurel fell into step beside me. We entered the house through a double door that led from the basketball court into a home gym that was larger than most apartments I'd lived in. Past the gym, we walked down a long corridor past several closed doors, and finally, Brantley led us into the first ballroom I'd ever seen inside of a house. The center of a ballroom featured a long table at which a man in a black suit and white gloves was busy setting a service for twelve. At the room's far end was a riser, which was where I assumed we'd be setting up. Sure enough, Brantley led us to the riser.

"You'll be here. I assume this space will be large enough?" he asked.

Bozeman stepped up onto the riser and did a quick loop around the area. I knew from experience that he was stepping off the space and also looking to make sure there were ample places to plug in our equipment. He stopped in the center of the riser, looked over at the rest of us, and smiled.

"This'll do fine," Bozeman said.

"Good, good. I'm glad you approve. I'm Hawthorne Harris." The voice boomed through the room, and when the group turned, they saw a short, portly man striding toward them. He wore a dark blue jogging suit that appeared to be more everyday wear for the man rather than athletic apparel.

"I'm Codi," I said, as I stepped forward and met the man halfway. He took my hand in his meaty paw and gave it a single shake before releasing it. His palm was moist, and when he let me go, I had to resist the urge to wipe my hand on my jeans while he was watching me.

"I assumed so. Are they the rest of the band?" he asked without looking at them, but rather just tipping his head in their general direction.

"Bozeman James and Laurel Preston. Two of the finest working musicians on the road today," I answered.

He smiled. "I'm looking forward to your performance. You come highly recommended. You need anything, you tell Brantley, and he'll take care of it." He turned to leave.

"Sir, excuse me, before you go."

Harris stopped and hesitated, and I could tell at that moment he wasn't used to people calling for his attention. To my surprise, he turned to face me rather than just walking away, even though the smile that stretched across his pudgy cheeks looked fake.

"Yes?" he asked.

"There's a matter of the band's fee. I hate to mention it now, but it's our policy to be paid on arrival. I'm sure you read it in the contract?"

Harris hesitated. "Sure, yes. Remind me the amount due?"

I told him, and to his credit, he didn't flinch when I gave him the number.

"Would cash be okay?" he asked.

"Sure. That would work," I said in a tone that suggested handling American greenbacks would be beneath me.

Harris fished a phone from his pocket and sent a text. "No problem. Jackie will be here in a couple of minutes with the money. Anything else?"

I didn't answer in the few seconds he allotted me, so he turned away and headed toward the door. He paused briefly, waved without looking back, then disappeared.

"Interesting man," I said.

"Mmm," Brantley answered.

The cell phone clipped into a case on his belt dinged, and he checked the message before returning his attention to me.

"I need to go. Please be set up by four. The caterer will make sure you're fed tonight and be ready to play at seven-thirty. Any questions?"

I didn't have any, so I shook my head.

"If you need anything, I'll be around somewhere." Like his boss, Brantley left the room.

"Friendly people," Laurel said, although I could hear a twinge of sarcasm in her voice.

"Can't always get the genuine fans when we do gigs like this. Hey, at least it's a nice place, right?" I said.

"That's true. I'm going to help Bozeman with the gear," Laurel said.

"I'll wait here for whoever Jackie is, and then I'll be there," I promised.

Unencumbered by activity, I stood where I was and watched the man setting the table. Even from where I was, I could tell it was a fancy affair based on the way the silverware shined. Another man joined the first and paid particular attention to any spots on the glassware before he set it on the table. In a way, I was glad I didn't get invited to dinner since not only did small talk before a show leave me feeling off my game, but also, I never learned which forks, spoons, and knives to use at the fancy feast. Give me a good old-fashioned barbecue picnic any day of the week. I much preferred the joy of eating corn off the cob rather than snails out of their shell.

A woman entered the room, and at first, I assumed she was Jackie, but then I noticed she dressed the same as the men at the table. They looked up from their work as she approached and greeted her warmly, and she folded the napkins into fancy shapes and set them atop each plate.

Another woman glided into the room, and I could tell this one wasn't part of the hired help. She was five-seven, just over a hundred pounds, and had a pair of designer sunglasses on top of her perfectly quaffed platinum blond hair. Her eyes were blue, as was the over-application of eye shadow, as were the tennis shorts she wore. Her teeth were the same white shade as her shirt, and her arms and legs were so tan it made me question her genealogical background. To her credit, as soon as she spotted me, a wide, genuine grin crossed her face, and she made a quick beeline to me.

"Codi Cassidy as I live and breathe! I'm Jackie May, and I'm so happy to make your acquaintance."

I extended my hand for a shake, but before I could even blink, she had wrapped both her arms around me in a hug that I doubted I could escape from on my own. Finally, I exhaled, and somehow, she drew me in closer.

"I'm such a big fan," she said when she finally released me.

"Thank you. It's always nice to meet a fan."

"When Hawth said he'd booked you for tonight, I got so excited. I listened to your CD over and over again. Are you going to play the whole thing for us?"

"About half," I answered. "My partner will play some of his songs too, and, of course, we'll play a bunch of covers. You have us booked for over three hours. That's a lot of time to fill."

"It sounds like it. I've been to lots of concerts where bands play for over three hours."

"Probably, but there were probably other bands on the bill too, right? Hardly anyone plays alone for three hours, unless it's the Boss. Don't worry. We'll give you a good show tonight. And if you have any requests, simply get my attention, and I'll see if we can work it onto the set list."

Jackie's grin got even wider. "Really? You'll do that for me?"

"Yep. Sure will."

I smiled, although I wasn't offering anything special to her. We took requests at all our shows, and usually we honored them since they were often the same requests from venue to venue. They were usually the classics by Willie, Dolly, Reba, Garth, and other mainstream country artists. Some requests would often venture into classic rock selections as well. Of course, there was always the one smart guy who would request *Free Bird*, which we more often than not honored. That one was always a showstopper.

"Oh, silly me, I forgot about your money," Jackie said as she slapped her palm against her head. "Hawth says I'd forget my own brain if God didn't cage it in my head."

"That's not a nice thing for your boss to say," I answered.

Jackie let loose with a laugh that was half hysterical and half donkey bray. She kept at it until she got a stitch in her stomach and had to stop and bend over to catch her breath.

"What did I say?" I asked.

Jackie straightened up and inhaled. "Oh, sugar, Hawth isn't

my boss, he's my fiancé."

That one took me by surprise. I felt my cheeks redden in embarrassment. "I'm so sorry. You see, I thought…"

"The same thing most people think when they see us together. It's okay. I'm used to it. And now you're probably thinking what someone like me would see in someone like him, other than the obvious big bank account, right?"

I didn't say anything, but I'm pretty sure my facial reaction gave it away. "No, that's not what I was thinking at all."

Jackie's grin returned. "You're the cutest little liar I've ever seen. I may be a blond, but I'm not an idiot. I know what people say about me, especially behind my back. Sure, I get I don't look like I would belong with someone like Hawth, but believe me, if you knew him like I know him, you'd fall madly in love with him, too."

I doubted it, since he was far beyond what I considered as my type, but I nodded and smiled, anyway.

"You're right. You can't really know about falling in love until you really get to know someone. I should have remembered that, since I've written about two dozen songs about it."

"Exactly. Now, about your fee for tonight." Jackie reached around to her back, and when her hand came back into view, there was an envelope in it, like a magician making an elephant appear from thin air. She held it out, and I hesitated for a second, then took it and went to shove it into my back pocket.

"Aren't you going to count it?" Jackie asked as her brow furrowed and for the first time, a frown appeared.

"I trust you. I don't need to."

Her shoulders slumped, and although it didn't seem possible, her frown deepened. I got the message, retrieved the envelope, opened it, and pulled out the stack of hundreds. In a dramatic display, I fanned through them, pretending I was counting, then felt something was off. I put the stack back together and paid closer attention when I actually did count them off the second time until I discovered there was indeed an error.

"Wait, there's a mistake here. There's twice as much as there should be." I went through the pile a third time, took from the top what the contract said they owed me, then held out the rest of the bills.

The grin returned to Jackie's mouth, and her eyes brightened again. "Gotcha!" She waved both hands in front of her. "I'm not taking that back. It's yours."

"It's too much. I can't take this."

Jackie looked offended. "Let me ask you this. Do you ever take tips? Or put out a hat or open your guitar case for passersby to toss pocket change into?"

I wondered if she realized that I was well past the point of my career where I had to play on random street corners, but I let it go.

"Rarely, and never when we have contracted gigs such as this," I said.

"What about T-shirts? Do you ever sell stuff like I've seen at other concerts? T-shirts and hats and stickers and whatever else?"

She had me there. "Yes. That we do. Except in cases like this. There's a difference between playing a private party, which we don't sell merch at, and playing a county fair where we do."

"Well, I'll make you a deal. You give me a T-shirt, autographed, and you consider that money payment for both. Come on. You're not going to win this argument. No one ever denies me of what I want."

I wanted to argue, and give the extra money back, but then I spotted Bozeman and Laurel lugging gear and I needed to jump in and help them. Besides, with the extra money, I knew we could afford to skip out on a gig or two if we wanted to.

"All right. You win. What size shirt do you want?"

CHAPTER FOUR

I placed the money back into the envelope and shoved it back into my pocket. I waved to Laurel, who was busy unpacking her fiddles and setting up her microphones, and I made my way through the corridors and back to the bus. When I finally arrived, I found Bozeman hauling amplifiers from the storage compartment under the bus and loading them onto a small cart.

"Everything go okay?" he asked when he sensed my approach.

"Why wouldn't it? I got the rest of the payment, so we're ready for tonight. Even got a bonus."

Bozeman raised an eyebrow at me. "Really? How much?"

"Over double the contract price," I said.

He smiled. "You're an excellent negotiator." Bozeman set an amp on the cart, but was unhappy with the placement, so he adjusted it to fit better.

"It was nothing to do with my skills. She says she's a fan, and she certainly enjoys throwing her man's money around. I'm going to drop this into the safe and I'll be right back out."

I boarded the bus and made my way to the equipment storage room. It was where we kept everything we didn't want to store under the bus. We were in the slow process of weeding through the room in order to convert it into a bedroom, since we wanted Laurel to have a place of her own other than the couch every night. Just inside the room was a built-in wall safe, not unlike the kind you'd find in a fancy hotel room, although ours was twice the size. I punched in the code, opened the safe, stowed the cash, and locked everything back up tight. A fleeting thought ran through my head, and I hesitated, trying to capture it again. Something was nagging at me, but I couldn't quite put a finger on what it was.

"Everything okay?"

The voice from nowhere startled me, and I backed right into the shelf behind me.

"Sorry. I didn't mean to scare you. Are you all right?" Bozeman asked.

"Of course. I thought you were outside," I said. I reached behind me and rubbed my lower back, where I'd caught the corner of something when I hit the shelf.

"Until I came in for the cable box, I was," Bozeman explained.

Since I was already standing where he needed to be, I turned around and grabbed the blue plastic milk crate that contained a variety of audio cables.

"Do you want all of them, or only a couple?"

"Hand me the box. I'd like to dig out some of the longer ones. Are you sure you're okay?"

"Yeah. I was just thinking about what to do with the kids tonight. I'm not sure I want them running around in the wild in this place. We certainly don't want them digging up the fairways or getting into the landscaping. I doubt Mr. Hawthorne Harris would be appreciative if Merle ate his prize roses."

"Probably not. Let them run free on the bus while we're gone. Once we get to the campground tonight, we can let them get some fresh air."

I nodded as I handed Bozeman the crate. "Good idea. Let's finish the load in and I'll come back and take care of them."

Bozeman turned left out of the room to head for the bus exit, but I turned right and stepped into my bedroom. For the gig, I needed my guitar, which was in its case, lying on my bed waiting for me. On top of the hardshell case was Gibson, who passed me the evil eye the second I entered the room.

"Hey, buddy, what's up with you?" I asked as I swept him up in my arms and sat down on the bed. "Are you trying to get me to stay home tonight? You know I can't do that. Mommy has to play the show so she can keep you in kibble."

I turned Gibson onto his back and gently scratched his belly. Before I'd even touched him, he purred, and the sound only increased the more I scratched him.

"Who's a good boy?" I asked as I watched a tiny puff of detached fur float into the air like a dandelion seed. After I gave Gibson a final scratch, I placed him on his usual spot, the tower of pillows at the head of my bed, and he did a slow circle and laid down. I reached for my guitar case, then stopped when I saw Gibson had left me a gift of enough cat fur on the front of my shirt to make another cat. Undaunted, I replaced the black T-shirt I was wearing with a clean black T-shirt exactly like the one I tossed on the floor. Satisfied, I was ready to face the world again, I grabbed the case and left the room.

When I got outside, I saw Bozeman had the cart loaded up and was ready for another trip.

"Can you grab my guitar?" Bozeman asked. He grunted once, then started pushing the heavy equipment-ladened cart toward the door.

I didn't answer, but I grabbed his road-worn guitar case and followed him with both our guitars in tow. It wasn't long before we reached the ballroom, and I set both guitars off to the side, then observed the stage setup. "We ready to go?"

Bozeman was rummaging through the crate of cables,

looking for the specific one he needed, and didn't bother to turn around when he answered. "I've got everything except the laptop."

I looked around the area, and sure enough, the laptop wasn't present. "I'll go back and get it. We need anything else?"

"I'm good," Bozeman answered.

"Laurel?"

Laurel was busy rosining up her bow, and shook her head, so I began the trudge back to the bus. I was almost past the catering truck when someone bounded down the stairs, bumped into me with a tray of salads, and knocked me onto my backside. Besides the jolt of my butt encountering the basketball court, I also jarred both wrists as I landed on my hands and felt a cold liquid run down the front of my shirt.

"Oh, twiddle, I'm so sorry."

I looked up and saw a chef from the food truck standing over me with half a tray of salads. The other three plates had shattered around me. The greens, assorted vegetables, and what smelled like Italian dressing became a part of my wardrobe.

She set the tray on the truck stairs, leaned over, and offered a hand. "Are you okay? I'm so sorry."

I took her hand, and she pulled me to my feet. My tail bone hurt, and my hands stung, but I didn't mention it. I hoped I could shake it off before the show started. "I'm fine, Heather," I said as I brushed off my shirt the best I could.

"How'd you know my name?" Heather asked as she pushed her plastic turquoise eyeglass frames up farther on her nose.

"Your name tag gave you away."

She giggled, then ran a hand through her pixie-cut light brown hair. "I guess so."

"You mind if I have the salad on the ground?" I asked.

"Odd question, but sure. I'm certainly not going to use it."

I smiled. "I've got a couple pets on board, and they love fresh veggies."

Heather's face brightened. She grabbed one of the salad plates from the tray and started adding the salad remnants that she picked up from the ground.

"I can get that," I offered.

"No. It's my fault. I'll do it. You might want to give this all a rinse before you give it to them. Get the dirt off and such."

I nodded in agreement as I helped by picking up the larger pieces of the broken plates. Together we worked in silence, and in a few minutes, the basketball court was back to mostly good playing condition. Heather handed me the plate of greens, and I handed her the broken plates.

"Again, I'm sorry. If I can make it up to you, please let me know how," she said.

I answered with another smile, turned, and returned to the bus. My first stop was in the kitchen, where I set a colander in the sink and thoroughly rinsed the vegetables. After the washing, I picked through them carefully to make sure there wasn't any unnatural debris in them. I kept them in the sink while I stripped off my shirt and went into the bathroom. There, I checked my image in the mirror, and it didn't surprise me when I saw my skin glistening where I got smeared with salad dressing. I sighed, fished a washcloth from the cabinet, and gave myself a quick wipe down. Once I felt cleaner, I returned to my bedroom, reapplied deodorant, and donned my third black T-shirt in less than an hour. I took a moment and grabbed my favorite long sleeved blue chambray shirt from my closet, then left the room. I found the laptop, which was on the dining table, then put my shirt on top of it so I wouldn't forget either item.

In the tiny kitchen there is a small metal grate inset into the floor, and I bent over and undid the clasp and opened the grate. I looked down into the hole and saw Dolly looking up at me.

"You two can have the run of the house for a while, okay? Be good, and don't bug Gibson too much, okay?"

I filled a plastic dish with water and placed it on the floor, and next to it I placed the rinsed vegetables on a plastic plate. As a last chore, I gathered up Gibson's dry food dish and locked it away in an upper cabinet.

Ready to leave the bus, I hesitated for a moment when I heard people speaking outside my bus.

"I'm telling you, I've had enough of him and his deals."

"Shh, someone will hear you."

I couldn't tell who was speaking, as their voices were low and were coming in through the cracked kitchen window.

"No one will hear me. There's no one else around. I'm telling you, Hawthorne Harris has screwed me over for the last time."

Curious, I wanted to see who was beneath my window, so I silently pulled over my step stool and set it into place next to the sink. I climbed the first step and leaned over to look out the window, but I wasn't high enough to see who was out there. Undaunted, I stepped on the second step. When I did, I leaned over a little too far and came into contact with the bottle of lemon scented dish washing soap that was right there. I realized I had contacted the bottle, and I looked down and watched it tip. Although I thought it was going to right itself, it continued moving and fell into the aluminum sink and made a sound like a gong.

"What was that?" a voice said.

"I don't know. Let's get back in there."

I jumped down from the stool and ran to the bus door, but by the time I made it outside, there was no one there.

Frustrated, I returned to the bus and passed through, shutting all the doors except my own, then gathered up my shirt and the laptop and left the bus, locking it behind me. I was already past the catering bus when I remembered the T-shirt for Jackie and backtracked to the bus. Once again, I fished the keys from my pocket and opened a storage compartment. I pulled out one of the plastic bins where we kept our merchandise, and I rummaged around in it until I found the correct size shirt. Quarry in hand, I closed everything up again and rejoined my friends.

"Took you long enough," Bozeman said as he looked up from his guitar. He plucked the D string, adjusted the tuning, then plucked it again to make sure it sounded pure.

"Sorry. I bumped into the caterer. I also had to change my shirt and feed the kids. Did I miss anything exciting?" I explained.

"Just Bozeman tuning that guitar for about an hour," Laurel said.

"And Red there has been playing Mozart stuff since you left. Good waste of a fiddle if you ask me," Bozeman teased.

"Come on, you two, play nice," I said as I made my way to a small table Bozeman had placed on the stage. I unfolded my laptop, booted it up, and called up the musical program I put together for the upcoming set. Most of the music was live, including my guitar, Bozeman's guitar, and Laurel's fiddle. When things really got popping, the computer added backing tracks for drums, bass, piano, and other assorted instruments. The vocals were live, and I found Laurel complimented my lead perfectly.

Once I had the program up and running, I connected the computer to the soundboard, and as simple as that, we were ready to go. At least we would be once I tuned my guitar. I opened the case and pulled out my Gibson. Although I could usually tune it by ear alone, I turned on the built-in tuner to move things along a little faster. Once I'd tightened the high E string, I plugged my guitar into my amplifier and set it on the stand, ready to go for the first number.

"Everyone else ready?" I asked.

Bozeman and Laurel nodded, almost in unison.

"Great. Any worries about the set?"

"Is there a set list?" Laurel asked.

I looked at the floor next to Laurel's microphone stand and

noticed there was no paper taped to the floor. "Oh, I'm sorry. I forgot to lay it down. I'll do that now."

Bozeman and I had played together for so long that we hadn't used a written set list in years. Since Laurel was new to the band, I promised I wouldn't leave her hanging in the dark wondering what song was next up. I went back to the laptop bag and pulled out several sheets. I found the three with today's date on them.

"Do you want these taped down, or do you want them loose?" I asked.

Laurel extended her hand. "I'll just take them and keep them on the stool next to my water. Thanks."

"Hey, listen. Can you guys do me a favor and keep your eyes open for me tonight?" I asked.

"What does that mean?" Laurel asked.

Bozeman moved over closer to us, leaned in, and whispered. "That means she's going to get us into trouble."

"Trouble? What kind of trouble?" Laurel asked, confused.

"Let's just say for someone so small, she can get into really large situations."

I was losing my cool, which was unusual for me. "Like last time, when you got accused of murder? That kind of trouble? Look, I overheard some people talking by the bus, and it sounded like they were unhappy with Hawthorne Harris."

"Unhappy how?" Bozeman asked.

"One of them mentioned how Harris had screwed them over on some deal," I said.

"Isn't he a real estate magnate? I'm sure he makes all kinds of deals that people are unhappy with," Bozeman said.

"Sardines," Laurel interjected.

"What?" I asked.

"Sardines," Laurel reported. "He's the great-grandson and only heir to the HH Sardine Company."

"How in the world do you know that?" I asked.

Laurel dug out her phone, opened the photos, and showed me a picture of the historical marker. I took the phone from her hand, blew up the picture, and read it aloud.

"HH Sardine Company established near this site in 1890 and quickly became the largest fishery and one of the largest companies in Northern California. Okay, but how did you tie that back to Hawthorne Harris?"

Laurel smiled. "It took me all of perhaps thirty seconds to bring up the HH Sardine Company website and see that Hawthorne Harris is the current CEO of the company. He's the fourth generation to run the company."

"What kind of dirty deal is there in the sardine business?" Bozeman asked.

It was a good question, and I didn't know. I shrugged.

"That's exactly what I thought," Bozeman said. "So why don't we just eat dinner, then play our gig, then pack up and go? Whatever his business is, it's not our business, so we should keep it that way."

"I agree with Bozeman," Laurel said. She stepped away from the group and placed the set list underneath the water bottle she kept on the wooden stool next to her station.

I took a moment, realized there was nothing at work except my overactive imagination. I smiled.

"That's fine by me. I don't like sardines, anyway."

CHAPTER FIVE

I gave a last look around at our setup and ran through the pre-concert checklist I always kept in my brain. It helped me to make sure everything was perfect. It also helped calm the jitters I always felt before every show. I heard someone approach, and I turned around and saw Brantley Wilson standing before me in the most outlandish getup I'd ever seen. The first thing I noticed were the knee-high leather boots, followed by the olive pants, green and brown tunic, and a green felt hat with a long red feather stuck on his head. Over his shoulder he carried a quiver, and in his left hand, he clutched a longbow.

I giggled. "Who are you supposed to be?"

Brantley rolled his eyes. "Robin Hood. No one mentioned that this is a costume party?"

"No. Had someone told me, I dress up like a spot-on Janis Joplin," I said.

"Doesn't matter. You won't be interacting with the guests much. If you and your compatriots would follow me to the main dining room. The caterer will feed you there, and you should stay there until it's time for the show."

We followed Brantley from the room and within two minutes he stepped aside and waved us into the dining room. Compared to the ballroom, the dining room seemed tiny, but it still held a table large enough to seat sixteen without touching elbows. At one end of the table, three place settings were waiting for us. Laurel and Bozeman took the seats across from each other, which left the head of the table for me. Since I was uncomfortable in that position, I gathered the dishes, silverware, and glasses, and moved them to the spot next to Laurel. I had just finished resetting the table when Heather entered, pushing a cart.

"Hello, again," Heather said to me as she stopped the cart near the table. She removed domes from the plates on the top shelf of the cart and placed salads before each of us.

"It looks much better on a plate," I said.

Heather slid me a sly smile. Since neither Laurel nor Bozeman knew the context, neither reacted to the comment.

"What would you like to drink with dinner? The other diners are having a specific wine with each course, but I can offer you about anything you'd like."

Although the wine sounded nice, all three of us opted for water. Heather had a pitcher on the cart's second shelf, and she filled Bozeman and Laurel's glass. She was filling mine when a loud gong reverberated throughout the room. Heather, startled, overfilled my glass, spilling the liquid on my lap.

"Oh my. I'm so sorry, again. I can't believe I did that," Heather said as she put down the pitcher and retrieved a towel from the cart. She started patting at my lap, but I took the towel from her.

"It's okay," I said while I sopped up the liquid. "It's only water. Hopefully, my pants will dry off before we hit the stage. What was that, by the way?"

"The gong? It's Hawthorne's way of letting everyone in the state of California know that he's ready for the next course."

"How many courses are they having that they need a

gong?" Laurel asked.

"Six. Hors d'oeuvre, soup, appetizer, salad, main course, and dessert," Heather said without thinking about it.

"How many are we having?" Bozeman asked as he picked up his fork.

"Three. Salad, main course, and dessert. Sorry about not giving you all six. Hawthorne likes to cut corners where he can."

"Not a problem," I said. "I never like to eat a lot before a show."

Heather smiled. "In that case, I'll make sure you have plenty to eat afterward. Would you like some fresh baked bread?"

That got Bozeman's attention. "How is that a question that anyone ever says no to?"

"This is California, honey. It would astonish you the things that people turn down. The one nice thing about Hawthorne Harris is that he always decides the menu, and it's always things that he likes. There are no special options for vegan, or gluten-free, or low-carb, or anything else. If a guest doesn't like what's being served, they either eat it anyway, or they're not invited back to any future parties. I have to go and supervise the service, and afterward I'll be right back with the bread. Again, I'm sorry about the water."

I smiled. "I'm just happy there's no soup course for us." Everyone laughed at that line, and Heather's cheeks turned pink with embarrassment. She dipped her head as she pushed the cart from the room.

Left alone, Laurel and I dug into our salads, even though Bozeman was already most of the way through his plate.

"Not a fan of olives?" I asked as I watched Laurel pick them from her salad.

"Not especially. As a kid I used to love them, and would eat them right out of the can, but one time I got a bad batch and got sick from them and haven't touched them since."

"That's fair," I said. "Do you mind if I take them?"

Laurel slid her plate over so it touched mine, and I used my fork to push the little pile onto the edge of my plate. When Laurel retracted her plate, I added my olives to her pile, and as I did, she watched with interest.

"What are you doing?" Laurel asked as I moved the last of them to the stack.

"I don't like olives either, but Dolly loves them."

Laurel and I both looked over at Bozeman, who was just putting his fork down on his clean plate.

"What? I like olives, too," he said as he wiped away a spot of dressing from his chin.

I heard the door open, and I looked over, expecting Heather with the bread, but it was Brantley.

"Mr. Harris has requested that you come and meet the guests," he said as he approached.

I wiped my mouth with the napkin and pushed my chair away from the table. "Okay. Let's go, gang."

Brantley cleared his throat, then leaned in toward me. "I'm sorry, he requested only you come and meet the guests."

I made a move to sit back down again, but Laurel stopped me by putting her hand on my arm. "Go ahead. I'm not big on schmoozing, and we both know how Bozeman feels about it."

I glanced over at Bozeman, who hadn't moved a muscle, other than to place his salad plate to the side to prepare for the next course.

"All right," I said, "let's go."

I followed Brantley back to the ballroom, and I had to stop for a moment when we entered the space so I could gather my thoughts and take in the sight. There were ten people seated around the giant table, and three steps behind them were what I assumed were servers, but they all seemed to be the same person. Each of them was female, had brown hair worn in a ponytail, and wore tuxedo pants, a stark white shirt, a purple cummerbund, and white gloves.

As I took another step toward the table, the gong rang out. It resounded even louder in the ballroom than it had in the dining room. With military precision, the servers stepped forward and cleared the hors d'oeuvre plates and silverware and left the room, silently, in a single file line.

"Hold up here for a moment," Brantley said to me. "Mr. Harris is particular about the service."

As requested, I stayed where I was and waited without speaking. Within three minutes, the server army returned, each carrying a large bowl of soup. I caught a glance at one of the bowls, and to me, it didn't even look appetizing. I always believed a soup needs either be hearty, like a nice stew, or needs to invoke memories, like the tomato with grilled cheese I got when I was a kid. The plain looking consommé looked like only the base of what a soup should be. The servers approached the diners, placed the soup before them, and stepped back to their original positions. To my amazement, concurrently, like they shared a hive mind. I noticed they changed the cummerbunds as well, from purple to a deep pink.

Once the sound of spoons contacting the bowls started up, Brantley took his seat at the table. I approached Hawthorne Harris, who sat at the head of the table. He dressed, of all things, like Julius Caesar. When he saw me coming, he stood, and I observed the full regalia he was wearing, from the laurel crown on his head, to the toga, to the leather sandals on his feet.

"Everyone. Everyone, your attention please. I'd like to introduce you to our entertainer for tonight, Codi Cassidy. She's a famous country star."

I heard one person applauding, and when I looked at the opposite end, I saw it was Jackie, who wore the outfit of Cleopatra. Right down to a rubber snake that she attached to her right shoulder. Hawthorne sent her a glare, so Jackie stopped the clapping and picked her spoon back up.

"Would you mind going around the table and saying hello

to my guests?" Hawthorne asked.

He took his seat without waiting for an answer, and I knew then he was one of those people who just expected people to do whatever was requested of them.

I slipped into performer mode, as easy as putting on a pair of shoes, and started making my way around the table.

Seated directly next to Hawthorne was someone I recognized right away. He wore a black Victorian high collar coat, black pants, red vest, and a black cape with a red border. It was the black slicked-back hair, pointy ears, and pointy teeth that gave it away.

"Count Dracula, I presume?" I said as I presented my hand.

The count stood, snapped the heels of his dress shoes together, took my hand, and kissed the top of it. "It's a pleasure to meet you Ms. Cassidy," he said in his best Bela Lugosi impression that, to be honest, wasn't that good. "My name is Claude Garrison. And may I present my friend, Amelia Brown?"

Amelia was in conversation with the person to her left, so Claude bent over and nibbled on her bare neck. That got her attention.

"Hey!" Amelia turned and slapped Claude playfully across the cheek. "Would you please stop doing that? It's getting annoying."

Dracula took his seat. "I just wanted to introduce you to Codi Cassidy."

"Charmed, I'm sure," Amelia said as she redirected her attention back to the man sitting next to her. Based on the pigtails, blue gingham dress, and the picnic basket at her feet with a toy cairn terrier sticking its head out, I assumed she was Dorothy Gale from *The Wizard of Oz*. Although upon first meeting she lacked any of the warmth that I associated with the character.

I moved on to the person she was talking to, who dressed as Frankenstein's monster. The monster, Danny Ewing, introduced me to his wife, Amy, who dressed as the Bride of Frankenstein.

Based on the way he looked at me and paid more attention to Amelia than to Amy, I could tell he was a player. I made a mental note to not get involved in his game, which wasn't hard since I didn't care for men with green skin and rubber bolts attached to their necks. I found Amy to be more interested in the alcohol that surrounded her place setting than she was in me. Based on her pout and glare, she wasn't happy with her husband, either so I moved toward the other end, where Jackie was excitedly waiting for me.

She took both my hands in hers and gave me the air kisses that the Europeans prefer, and when she did, the snake on her shoulder nuzzled my cheek.

"Thank you for coming to say hello. My outfit is out there, isn't it? Can you guess who I am?" Jackie said giddily.

"Yeah. You look great. Just like the real Cleopatra. I'd better say hello to the others so I can get back to my band. I'll talk to you later, okay?"

Jackie let me loose from her grip, so I moved onto the next person, who, out of everyone, looked the least like she was at a costume party. She wore a long white dress, and a white shawl covered her shoulders.

"Hello, I'm Codi Cassidy," I said as I offered my hand.

"Helen Troy," the woman said as she put down her soup spoon and gave me a quick shake.

"Helen of Troy? That's a pretty obscure costume, I might say."

The redhead laughed, then dabbed her mouth with a napkin. "No. My parents, Deana and Armond Troy, were both history buffs and thought it would be hilarious to name their only daughter Helen. I hate costume parties, so I just throw on a nice dress and go as my namesake. Saves me a lot of effort."

I nodded, and Helen returned her attention to the soup, so I assumed the conversation between us was over. I said a brief hello to Brantley, who was next in line, then I moved to the woman seated to his left. Before I got there, she stood.

"Codi. It's so good to see you again. It's been a long time. You don't recognize me, do you?"

She was a black woman and was a good six inches taller than me. Since she wore dark blue sorcerer's robes adorned with stitched silver stars, a tall, pointed hat to match, and a long white beard, I couldn't pinpoint if I'd met her before.

"You're a wizard?" I asked.

"Merlin. It was Loren's idea." She pointed a thumb at Loren, who, I guessed, had decked out like King Arthur. The woman took off the hat, then removed the beard. I saw she was a pretty woman, but other than that, I didn't recognize her.

"Viola. Viola Park. I was your dad's partner in Denver for a couple of years. Don't you remember me?"

I reached back into the recesses of my mind, trapped a memory, and grinned.

"You used to sneak me chocolate bars all the time."

Viola nodded, then pulled me into a hug. "It's so good to see you again. How are you?"

"I'm good. What are you doing out here? Are you not with the Denver Police Department anymore?"

"No. Once I got my detective's shield, I hit the glass ceiling, so I went searching for other positions. I'm the head dog out here."

"No kidding?"

"That's right. Police chief," she said.

"That's amazing," I admitted.

"How is your dad?"

"Good. He retired from the force a few years ago." I was about to expand on the small talk when the gong rang. Without a word, Viola retook her seat.

"You can go."

I turned around and saw it was Brantley speaking to me.

"Go. Back to your friends. We don't want to keep you any

longer."

I hesitated for a moment, then stepped back from the table. The servers had waited for me to leave, and as soon as I headed toward the door, they progressed through the act of clearing away the soup bowls. By the time I got to the door, the servers were only a step behind me, so I moved to the side and let them pass. I didn't want to impede whatever the next course was.

I backtracked my way back to the dining room, where I found Laurel and Bozeman in the middle of their main courses. At my place was a stainless-steel dome, under which I assumed my dinner was.

"There you are," Laurel said. "We didn't know when you were coming back, so we dug in. Hope you don't mind."

"Of course not." I lifted the dome. Underneath was a Cornish game hen, a bed of wild rice, and two roasted carrots. "Did Heather ever bring the bread?"

Bozeman grunted and passed the plate on which sat three dinner rolls. I took one, found the butter, and lathered up the roll. Then I went to work on picking apart the miniature chicken.

"What's it like in there?" Laurel asked as she scooped up a forkful of rice.

"Just your average costume party for rich people," I answered.

Daintily, I removed a leg from the hen and took a bite. I wasn't normally one for fancy food, but I had to admit, it was delicious.

"I've never been to a costume party," Laurel said. She was only half finished with her meal but pushed her plate away. "I don't know why people think these mini chickens are so great. I think they're way more trouble than they're worth."

"Bozeman didn't have any trouble with it."

Laurel and I looked at Bozeman, who was nibbling away the last of the meat on a tiny wing. On his plate was a small pile of bones. He looked at us, then added the wing to the pile, wiped his mouth, and drank some water.

"They're all right by me," Bozeman said. "Although I'd prefer it fried."

The gong sounded before anyone could say another word.

"That's a little much," Laurel said.

"You should see what it triggers. The servers have this well-coordinated dance they do to remove the plates and bring in the next course. It's quite fascinating to see, like they're all programmed robots. Although, it's also a bit disconcerting. Trust me, though, I'd rather have dinner with the two of you."

I finished half of my meal and pushed it aside. Although everything was delicious, I didn't want to fill up too much before the gig.

"I wonder how much longer we'll be stuck in here," I said.

Neither Laurel nor Bozeman answered me, but fifteen minutes later, the gong sounded. I had lost track and didn't know if it was the fifth course or sixth, but I was certain someone would come to tell us at some point or another.

CHAPTER SIX

Forty-five minutes later, after we'd each eaten a slice of Loren's excellent pie, Brantley stepped halfway into the room and motioned for us to follow him.

"Now is the time for your sound check. I want you to make sure that everything is perfect for your performance. Mr. Harris is very particular and won't stand for any problems during the concert."

"Okay," I said. What I didn't say was that there were problems all the time during performances. There were a few dozen things that could go wrong during a show. A guitar string might break, a light bulb in the lighting rig may pop, an amplifier could decide to whine and emit some feedback. Once I forgot to plug in the laptop, and I ran out of battery right in the middle of a Reba McEntire medley. The most likely thing to happen would be that Bozeman would drop several guitar picks over the course of the night. I asked him once why he dropped so many during a show, and he said he played with them until they didn't feel right anymore. The odd thing is, he'll pick them up from the floor after the concert and use them for the next gig, almost as if the act of falling to the floor returns the original mojo to them.

Brantley escorted us to the ballroom. The servers, now in dark green cummerbunds that matched Brantley's tights, were busy clearing the table. On the far side of the room, two women in tuxedos were setting up a portable bar.

"You have a half an hour to get ready. All the guests are in the drawing room," Brantley said, bored with us. He gave us a dismissing wave, then let us be.

"Drawing room? I don't even know what that is," Bozeman said as he stepped onto the riser and started turning on the sound equipment.

"It's something we don't have room for on the bus," I said as I took my place behind the microphone.

I picked up my guitar, gave it a couple of strums to check the tuning, then started playing the first song that jumped into my head, which happened to be an old Willie Nelson classic. As I worked my way through *Angels Flying to Close to the Ground*, Bozeman left the stage and walked to different spots in the room to check on the acoustics. Twice he came back and adjusted the soundboard, then he settled into a chair along the farthest wall from us next to a row of floor to ceiling windows.

When I finished, I received a smattering of applause, and looked over and learned it was the bartenders giving me love.

"Thank you," I said. I waved to them and removed my guitar from my shoulder.

"Laurel, play something for us," Bozeman called out without moving from his chair.

Laurel stepped forward, and after a quick mic check, launched into a short classical piece on her fiddle. It wasn't anything that would fit into our normal set, but I have to admit, I loved to listen to her play anything. She was so talented; I felt lucky to have her as a part of the band. When she finished, she got more of an ovation from the bartenders than I had gotten, and I joined in as well.

"Do a mic check on mine," Bozeman requested.

I picked up Bozeman's guitar and from his setup started the song I'd just finished, but I only made it through half of the song before Bozeman stood and waved me off.

When I returned Bozeman's guitar to the stand, and I turned back around, a large sonic boom rocked the room. I looked over at Bozeman, but he was staring out of the window. Laurel and I crossed the room and joined him.

The large windows faced west, and beyond a hundred yards of well-manicured lawn, the property ended at the cliff side. Out in the Pacific, there were large black clouds forming, blotting out the setting sun. Although dark was falling, I noted the raging whitecaps on the waves.

"Storm moving in," Bozeman said.

Just as the words left his mouth, a bolt of lightning appeared over the ocean and a few seconds later, another peal of thunder rumbled through the house.

"I guess so," Laurel said.

I saw Brantley walk toward us in the window's reflection, and he stopped by my side and looked out the window just as another flash lit up the sky.

"Are you ready to go?" Brantley asked.

"Yep. We're all set," I answered. "Are we going to be okay here? Seems like a terrible storm coming."

Brantley smiled to assure me. "We'll all be fine. They built this house like a fortress, and if we lost power, the emergency generator would kick on so fast you wouldn't notice the disruption."

Brantley left us and I watched his reflection in the mirror as he walked to the bar and ordered a drink. By the time I'd turned around, he'd already downed it, and was holding his glass out to the bartender for a refill.

"I guess it's going to be one of those nights." I shook my head as I walked in his direction.

By the time I'd reached the bar, Brantley had retreated with his drink.

"What can I do for you?" the bartender asked.

"Do you have any bottled water for us? Preferably room temperature?" I asked.

"Not back here, but Stacy can get you some. How many do you need?"

"Six will do for now."

The bartender turned and addressed her counterpart, and Stacy hustled from the room. "I like that song you played before. I've always been a Willie fan," the bartender said.

"Thank you, um," I hesitated as I looked for a name tag, since I always liked to address people properly. I didn't see one, though.

"Ashley," the bartender filled in as she smiled at me.

"Thank you, Ashley." I smiled back.

Ashley looked over my shoulder and her eyes got brighter, and I knew what that meant. Bozeman was right behind me.

"Think I might get a beer from you?" he asked, putting down a southern drawl like a thick blanket.

"Sure thing. We have a bottle or tap, depending on what you'd like," Ashley started.

As Ashley ran through the options with Bozeman, I turned away and headed back to the stage.

"Does that always happen?" Laurel asked. "He steps into the picture and every female eye around gets diverted his way?"

"Usually. You'll get used to it, though. And to be honest, sometimes it's nice that the attention goes to him."

Stacy came back, wheeling in an entire case of water on a small hand truck. She parked it by the stage, ripped through the plastic, and pulled out two bottles. "Here you go."

I took the two bottles and put them on Bozeman's stool, then grabbed a couple more and handed them to Laurel. Finally, I took two more, cracked the seals, and put them next to my station.

"I can leave the rest of these here, but I'll have to find a tablecloth or something to cover them," Stacy said. "Mr. Harris doesn't like any trash sitting about."

"I can put it behind our gear back here. No one will notice," I offered.

Stacy smiled, lifted the rest of the case, and put it on the stage. "Thanks," she said, then she turned and wheeled the dolly from the room.

"You need help with that?" Laurel asked, pointing to the bottles.

I smirked at her. "No, but thank you."

I picked up the remaining six bottles in the case and moved the whole thing to the back of the stage, where we'd stacked up our cases and other gear. I dropped it behind Bozeman's guitar case and stepped back to my position.

"Oh, boy," Laurel said. "Live one coming in hot."

I looked up and saw Jackie coming toward us. Her dress tapered inward the farther down it went, so she had to do a quick shuffle to get to us.

"Are you ready to go? I'm so excited!" she screeched.

"I can tell," I said. "Oh, here's something I promised you." I moved back to the gear and found the shirt I'd pulled out for her. "Would you still like me to sign it?"

"Of course!" she blurted, as if it were even a question.

Laurel did a half eye roll and handed me a marker. I set the shirt flat on my stool, removed the cap, and signed the shirt. "To Jackie, with love, Codi Cassidy," I said aloud as I wrote.

I returned the pen to Laurel as I gave the ink a few seconds to dry, then I handed the shirt to Jackie.

Jackie opened the shirt and stared for a moment at the signature, as if she hadn't believed her eyes when I'd signed it a few seconds ago. She squealed with joy.

"I'm going to go put this on right now."

"I don't think it will fit over your snake," I said. "And it doesn't go with your pretty dress. You should save it for another time."

She pouted for a couple of seconds, then her smile returned. "Okay. I'll go put it in my room, so it doesn't get lost or dirty."

"Good idea," I said. She didn't need my permission, but she seemed to appreciate it, and shuffled away with her prize in her hand.

"You sure made her day," Laurel said. "Can I have your autograph, too?"

I thought about giving Laurel a punch to the shoulder, but then the doors opened wide, and the costumed guests started filling the room. Bozeman noticed it as well, so he stopped flirting with the bartender and joined us on stage. Bozeman and I donned our guitars, and we both put on our hats to complete our stage personas.

The guests filed in and half of them headed to the bar. The other half took seats at two-person tables that replaced the main table, which the staff had disassembled and turned into side tables that lined the walls.

Once everyone had drinks in their hands and seemed to be settled in, we prepared to jump right into our set. I began a rhythm count and got as far as two before Hawthorne Harris scrambled to his feet and started waving his hands at me.

"Wait! Wait! I want to say a few words!"

Since he was the one footing the bill, I moved back from the mic and made way for him. As he stepped onto the riser, his sandaled foot caught the lip and he fell forward. I thought he would slam right into my Gibson, but Bozeman caught him before he did a face plant. Harris approached the mic like it didn't even happen.

"Thank you again everyone for coming to the party tonight, and thanks for playing along with the costume theme. There's a prize for the best costume, and I'll announce who the winner is later."

As Harris spoke, I looked around the room to catch the reaction of those listening. Brantley was finishing yet another cocktail, and based on the way he eyed the bar, I assumed he wanted a refill. Danny Ewing stood directly behind Helen Troy, and I noticed by his line of sight that he was more interested in her backside than Harris' speech. Meanwhile, his wife was clearly watching Danny watching Helen. If it were physically possible for steam to come from someone's head, Amy would be hot enough to power a locomotive. The rest of the room, except for Jackie, was watching the speech, mostly with disinterest.

The guests clapped, so I brought my attention back to Hawthorne, who was holding a hand toward me. I gave him my stage smile, shook his hand, and thanked him. He left the stage and took his seat. When he did, three servers appeared from nowhere, each with a tray of champagne flutes. Once each of the guests had a glass, Hawthorne gave a toast, and everyone drank. Then he waved at me, and I took that as a sign to start the show.

I turned around to face the band. "Ready? Again?"

Laurel and Bozeman both nodded, so I faced the audience, began the rhythm count again, then swung into the set. As usual, we started with a couple of songs from my first album, and then Bozeman performed one of his. The first few songs we always played acoustically so that the audience knew it was really us behind the guitars and the vocals. After that, I kicked on the computer to use the backing tracks.

We were halfway through our fifth song. Bozeman was crooning about having *Friends in Low Places*, when I spotted a flash of lighting that cracked loud enough to be heard over our music.

"Holy crap," someone exclaimed. Although it was a male voice, I couldn't tell where it came from.

Our speakers lost sound, and the lights in the room flickered, then dropped out. A woman screamed. Another bolt of lightning flashed outside the window, and a few seconds later, a rumble of thunder shook the house.

"Don't worry folks. The lights will be on in a second," Hawthorne said. As if on cue, two counts later, the lights popped back on as bright as before. "Nothing to worry about. That's why we have a generator. Let's get back to the party. Bring back the music!"

I looked out into the crowd and caught lots of expectant eyes staring back at me. When I did a mic check, I discovered my first problem when I heard nothing from my amp. I stepped from mine to Bozeman to apologize. "I'm sorry, but it's going to take us a couple of minutes to get back to the show. We need to do a quick equipment check to make sure everything is good. I promise, it will only be a brief break."

Several from the crowd moaned at the announcement, and I could tell from the daggers Hawthorne Harris was shooting at me from his eyes that he wasn't happy. But what could I do? Electronics and power snafus have never gone together well.

"Let's get back up and running, as fast as we can, okay?" I said to Laurel and Bozeman.

I did a fast check of my amp and guitar, and determined my problem was the power strip I used popped a fuse. After I reset it, I moved over and checked the computer. Something had happened to it, since the screen displayed a black screen with a blue circle spinning around. Since my hardware technical knowledge only spanned as far as rebooting the machine, I pressed the power button until the display darkened. I counted to ten in my head before I turned on the laptop. I waited with bated breath until the screen popped up and informed me that something terrible had happened, but it asked if I wanted to continue as normal. If only such things occurred in real life. I opted for booting up as usual, then checked on how the others were doing.

"How's everything?" I asked Laurel first since she was the closest one to me.

"All good," she answered. "It looks like Boze has a problem, though."

I looked over at Bozeman, and he displayed the red ears he got every time he was getting frustrated. I joined him to see if I could help.

"What's going on?" I asked.

"Amp is dead," he answered.

"Did you check the fuse?"

"I was about to."

Bozeman bent over and popped the fuse out and passed it to me. I held it up to the light and determined it had fried.

"Yep. It's dead. Got a spare?" I asked.

"On the bus," Bozeman answered.

I looked out the window in time to see another flash of lightning, and it was raining hard.

"I don't suppose you brought a spare amp?"

Bozeman smiled at me. "Of course. It's also on the bus."

I handed him the fuse. "Looks like you're going to get wet, my friend. You have the keys? I locked it when I left."

Bozeman checked his pocket, nodded, and rushed from the room. I turned around to find Brantley waiting for me.

"What's the delay?" he asked. I could tell by the way he slurred his speech that he'd been drinking too much.

"We're almost ready to go. We've got a blown fuse, and a couple of other things to check. Give us ten minutes, and we'll be back at it."

Brantley glared at me for a second. "Okay, but you need to know that Mr. Harris isn't happy."

He left without waiting for a response. That was probably for the best because I could feel the snark monster that lives in my brain wanting to take over the conversation for me. Instead, I returned to the computer, saw everything had booted up as normal, so I called up the program. Once I did a quick check to see it was working fine, I returned to my stool and had a seat while I waited for Bozeman. He appeared five minutes later, dripping wet, with a new fuse in hand. A couple of minutes later, we were back in business.

"Sorry for the delay, everyone. We're back. Bozeman here is going to take the last song from the top."

Bozeman started playing the opening riff of the song, inhaled a breath to start the lyrics, and the dinner gong sounded. It was a distraction, sure, but we were seasoned musicians used to distractions, so we kept on playing. Out in the audience, I saw Hawthorne call Claude Garrison over, and based on the body language and the flying arm gestures, I could tell Claude was getting a reaming. Near the beginning of the first chorus, the gong sounded again, and Hawthorne seemed to get even angrier. I could hear an argument brewing, but since I was singing backup in the chorus, I couldn't make out the words. He pointed at Claude, pointed at the door, and a millisecond later, Claude the vampire headed for the exit.

Things settled down, and when Bozeman finished the song, he got a nice round of applause.

I stepped up to my mic. "I'm going to take things back, and here's a nice slow dance number, so if you want to grab a partner and hit the floor, do so."

I took a moment to swallow a mouthful of water while people paired up, then I stepped up to the microphone. Bozeman started the opening riff, and I had barely opened my mouth to sing the first word when the lights went out again.

The woman who had screamed the first time screamed again. Clearly, she wasn't a fan of surprises, summer storms, or the dark. The dinner gong sounded five times in a row, and thirty seconds later, the lights came on again.

There was another scream, this time from a different woman. When I looked out at the audience, I saw Hawthorne Harris face down on the floor, with a bright red spot widening on the back of his white emperor robes.

CHAPTER SEVEN

The lights stayed on for a scant fifteen seconds before they dropped out again. The scream returned.

"Stop that," a woman ordered. Even in the dark, I recognized Viola's authoritative tone. "Nobody move, stay exactly where you are," she said, loud enough for everyone in the room to pick up over the oncoming peal of thunder.

The voices stopped. All I noticed were a couple of echoing footsteps, and then nothing but a loud sob. The lightning flashed again, and for the briefest of seconds I saw the people in the room standing still, as if they were statues.

"Everyone hold where you are," Viola said.

Without thinking about it, I counted the passing seconds in my head, and when I reached forty-nine, the lights flickered twice and came on. Although I expected them to pop off again, this time, they brightened and remained. I looked around the room and detected that most people had complied with the order to stay where they were. Even so, I noticed Danny had taken a seat, and Helen had sprawled out on the floor as if she'd fainted.

Viola took off her pointed hat and fake beard. With haste,

she rushed to Hawthorne's side. She kneeled down and felt for a pulse. When she didn't find one, she shook her head and unzipped her robes in search of her cell phone. She dialed a number, held the phone to her ear, and waited. After a moment, she looked at the phone and shoved the phone back into the pocket of her black jeans.

Brantley stepped over to her, and without looking at the body, he asked the pertinent question we all wanted the answer to. "Is he alive?" Brantley asked.

"No," Viola answered. "I need to call this in, but my cell isn't going through."

"911?" Brantley asked.

"That will do," Viola said.

She moved away from the scene and stripped off the wizard's robes. Along with the black jeans, she wore a black shirt as well. On her belt I spotted her badge and gun and assumed, like my dad, she never considered herself off duty.

Brantley retrieved his phone and tried to make the call, then gave up and put it away. "I can't get through to anyone, either."

From my vantage point, I saw a couple of other people try to call for help, but like Viola and Brantley, no one got through to anywhere.

"Is there a land line?" Viola asked.

Brantley led her in my direction, and they stopped at a wall phone right next to the stage. Odd that I hadn't noticed it before, since I was usually aware of my environment like that.

Viola picked up the receiver, placed it to her ear and hung up right away. "It's dead, too." She gave a weak smile. "Sorry. Bad choice of words, considering the circumstances."

"Trying to call for help?" I asked.

Viola nodded at me. "Cell service and land lines are both out."

"Bozeman can drive into town and get help," I offered.

I looked over at Bozeman, who was giving me the

impression that he didn't appreciate me volunteering him for things, especially during heavy rain.

"Don't bother," Brantley said. "Once we lost power, the compound would have gone into automatic shutdown, and the gates would have closed and locked. Someone would have to walk to the guard shack and perhaps they would get help in here."

"You up for a stroll, Bozeman?" I offered.

Much to Bozeman's delight, Viola answered the question. "I don't want anyone leaving the building at this point."

She turned her attention back to Brantley. "So, you're saying we're stuck here?" Viola asked.

"Well, only until the power gets fully restored and security clears the compound," Brantley answered.

"How long will be that be?" Viola asked. As the last syllable left her lips, the lights flickered again, but fortunately, they didn't go out.

Brantley's gaze focused on the crystal chandelier in the middle of the room, and when it flickered again, his eyes shifted back to Viola. "I'd say at least until this storm passes. Maybe longer if there are any lines down or any other disruptions to the power grid."

"I guess we're here for the duration," Viola said. "Can you grab me a notebook and a pen from somewhere?"

Brantley looked at her for a moment, then averted his eyes. "No problem. I'll be right back."

Viola didn't move as Brantley left the room. She turned to me.

"What did you observe?" she asked as she took a step closer to me.

"Not really much of anything," I answered.

Viola smiled at me. "You? Codi Cassidy? There was a reason your dad always called you eagle eye. You never missed a thing. Remember the game we used to play when you'd come over to my place?"

"I remember." I wasn't lying. Every time my dad and I visited Viola's place, she moved items around in her living room for me to notice. It was never anything major, like rearranging all the furniture, but rather something minor, like moving a ceramic figurine from one shelf to another or exchanging pictures on a wall. At the end of the visit, she'd asked if anything seemed different, and I listed off what changes I caught and for each one I got correct, she'd give me a cookie. I always enjoyed those well-earned treats on the way home.

"You've always had a better eye for detail than anyone I've ever known. Now tell me, what did you notice?"

"There's not much to tell. We were just starting a new song, the dinner gong rang, the lights went out, the lights came back on again, and Hawthorne was lying dead on the dance floor."

"Did you see anything else?" she asked.

I smiled. "I know I have excellent observation skills, but even I can't see in the dark. You know I'm not a wolf, right?"

Viola sighed at the response. "What about before the room went dark? Can you tell me if you spotted anything unusual?"

"Not really. Danny Ewing seemed to be getting sloppy drunk, which, to me, isn't unusual. I always spot a few people in the crowd who have had too many. Oh, and Jackie wasn't back yet."

Viola looked around the room. Jackie was still nowhere in sight. "How long has she been gone?"

I tried to give it my best estimate. Since I had focused on the show, she could have returned and left again. "Twenty or thirty minutes?"

Voila jotted the information into the notebook. "You know where she had gone to?"

"I gave her one of my T-shirts and autographed it for her. She told me she was going to run it to her room so nothing would happen to it."

Viola nodded. "Can either of you tell me anything more?"

Laurel and Bozeman were both standing within four feet of us and had overheard the entire conversation.

"I didn't. I was paying more attention to Codi than anything else," Laurel explained. "Since I'm relatively new to the band, and this is my first performance with them."

"I got nothing, either. I had my eyes closed most of the time," Bozeman said.

Viola gave him a look I remembered from my childhood when I said anything she didn't believe. "Seriously?"

"Probably," I jumped in. "He goes into this kind of Zen state when he's playing and it's so automatic that he often literally keeps his eyes closed while he's playing. Especially if he's only playing guitar and not singing."

"Craziest thing I've ever heard," Viola said.

Bozeman shrugged. "It's normal for me. Guitar is mostly muscle memory since I've been playing so long."

"You've got company headed your way," I said.

Viola turned around and saw Brantley rushing toward us, carrying the supplies she'd asked for. Without a word, he handed her three notebooks and a handful of pens, then turned and headed toward the bar.

Viola took a notebook, then handed it to me. "Look, I have a concern that since we can't get outside help that this crime scene will turn into a contaminated mess. I need to start documenting everything and get a jump on what happened here. Can you help me out? Maybe interview the staff? And Bozeman, could you find a way to seal off the perimeter around the body to make sure no one messes with it?"

"Why not just seal off this room?" I asked. "Keep everyone out. That would keep the body from being disturbed."

"It would also mean I'd have suspects running free all over the house. No way. I want everyone in this room where I can keep an eye on them until I get reinforcements."

"Suspects?" Laurel asked. "We're all suspects?"

Viola looked at Laurel like she'd just said the silliest thing ever. "I wouldn't be as concerned if Hawthorne had dropped dead of a heart attack or even got struck by lightning, but he didn't. Someone shot him in the back. And yes, everyone is a suspect, except, I believe, you three."

I'd heard that before. Being on stage performing in front of a crowd always provided an excellent alibi for any crime. Except, occasionally, messing up the lyrics to a George Strait song.

"Okay. Is everyone in and willing to help me?" Viola asked.

I agreed, as did Bozeman.

"What should I do with the body?" Bozeman asked.

"Cover it up with something, like a blanket, and somehow cordon it off so no one will mess with it," Viola said. "Then keep a close eye on it, so no one goes near it."

"What about footprints and fingerprints?" he asked.

Viola smiled. "You've watched one too many television shows. Don't worry about the footprints, unless you see a bloody one. All of us in here have been tromping all over the place all night. So has the staff."

Bozeman glanced over at Laurel. "Can you give me a hand?"

"Sure. What do you want me to do?" she asked.

"Find something to cover the body with, and I'll take care of the perimeter."

"Wait until I give you the word to cover it. I want to get some pictures first," Viola ordered.

Bozeman nodded in understanding. Voila and I stood aside as Bozeman grabbed the cable crate and headed toward the body. Laurel made her way to the side of the room, where the staff had shoved a table against the wall. She removed a giant candelabra from the center, placed it on the floor, and stripped the tablecloth from it.

Bozeman arranged four chairs, one at each corner of

Hawthorne's body. Then he used the microphone and amplifier cables to block off the body. When he finished, the area looked like a homemade wrestling ring.

"Okay. Let's get to work," Viola said. "Like I said, you take the staff, like the servers and the bartenders, and I'll handle the guests at the party. Take pictures of everything you think is pertinent and get witness statements and contact information for everyone you talk to."

Without waiting for an answer, she turned to leave, but I knew I had to stop her. "Viola, wait."

She pirouetted and waited. "Earlier today, I heard a couple of people talking outside my bus."

"About what?"

"I couldn't tell for sure. The voices were quiet, but I overheard them talking about some poor deals that they'd been through with Hawthorne."

Viola subconsciously scratched her temple with a pen. "Bad business usually makes for likely motives."

I smiled. "My dad always said love and money were behind ninety percent of the crimes he'd investigated."

"That percentage sounds about right. Do you know who was talking?"

I shook my head. "No. Sorry. Other than the sentence that caught my attention, and the loud shush that quieted everything down, I couldn't tell."

"Could you at least give me a clue? Man? Woman? Accent? Speech impediment?"

I hesitated for a moment before answering so I could think for a moment to see if anything came to mind. "No."

"Okay. Hopefully, we'll figure that out. Grab your phone and let's go to work."

We stepped from the stage, and I followed Viola to Hawthorne's body. Once there, Viola retrieved her phone and snapped pictures from every angle. I thought she'd want to roll

Hawthorne over, and I was there, ready to volunteer Bozeman's services again. But when she finished, she nodded at Laurel.

"Okay, cover him," Viola said.

Laurel grabbed the tablecloth and passed one end to me. Bozeman disconnected a cable to give us access to the body, and we stepped in and gave Hawthorne a shroud. We stepped away, Bozeman reconnected a cable, then pulled up a chair and sat down, ready to do the next part of his duty.

I turned to ask Viola a question and saw she'd stepped away and was busy taking photos of the room, including all the people in it. I did a quick scan for all the people I'd remembered meeting, and everyone, including Ashley and Stacy were at the bar, which had suddenly turned into a popular place. Except Jackie. Jackie remained missing from the room, and I wondered where she'd been all that time. I also wondered how she'd react when she learned her meal ticket was gone forever. Then my thoughts passed to his will, and I wondered who would be inheriting the estate and whatever fortune he had. I let that one pass and assumed it had crept into Viola's mind already. This certainly wasn't her first rodeo.

"What should I do?" Laurel asked when she noticed Viola seemed too busy to answer the question.

I thought about it for a second. "Can you lend me your phone? I left mine on the bus and she wants me to take pictures of people I talk to."

"Where's yours?" Laurel asked as she pulled her phone from her back pocket.

"On the desk in my bedroom," I answered, even though I'd just told her where it was. I remained horrible about always carrying it with me, even though Bozeman continued to stress the importance of having it on my person at all times. Even so, I liked to disconnect from the world, so it spent more time in my bedroom than in my pocket.

Laurel fidgeted with the phone for a moment, then passed

it to me. "I've turned off the lock screen, so you have access to anything you need."

Since her phone was different from mine, I pushed a button to check it, and the screen lit up immediately, displaying her apps. I saw the camera icon, pressed it, and it opened fine.

"You're not worried about me finding all your secrets in here?" I asked.

"I would be if I had any," she answered right away. "What do you need me to do?" she repeated.

I glanced around the room. Someone had revived Helen and gotten her into a chair where she currently nursed a drink. Everyone had clustered into small groups of two or three, and Viola had Loren off to the side and I could tell the interrogation had begun.

"I think you should keep alert and help Bozeman guard the scene."

"He can't handle that himself?" Laurel asked.

I shook my head and pointed behind her. Laurel turned around and looked at Bozeman. He had found a second chair to put his feet on, then pulled his hat down and seemed to be in the midst of a nap.

"Seriously?" Laurel asked.

I smiled. "We could be in the middle of a zombie apocalypse, and he would probably ask someone to wake him when things got really bad and head off to slumberland. Don't worry, if there's trouble, he'll wake in an instant and will stand ready to deal with anything."

"Is there anything else I should do?" Laurel asked. She moved a few feet away, retrieved a chair for herself, pulled it close to me, and sat.

"Yeah. Sit with your back to the wall and remember, someone in here is a murderer," I answered.

A look of realization flashed into her eyes, a look that told me she grasped finally what was happening. She opened her mouth to ask a question, closed it, rose, and moved her chair next to the wall where she'd retrieved the tablecloth. She sat literally with her back to the wall, and I don't think a gallon of black coffee would make her more awake and intense than she looked at the moment.

I returned to her and grabbed her hand. "It'll be okay. Just stay where there are lots of people around, and you'll be fine."

Laurel pointed toward Hawthorne. "The group didn't prevent that from happening."

She had a valid point there.

"Okay. Then also hope the lights stay on," I said.

She gave me another smile, one I suspected she flashed to convince herself that all would turn out well. I gave her hand another squeeze.

"You'll be fine," I said. A final squeeze, and I let her go. I turned to leave.

"Hey, Codi?"

I turned back around. "Yeah?"

"Be safe."

It was my turn to smile. "Of course. What's the worst that can happen?"

Laurel didn't answer. Instead, she rolled her eyes at me. In response, I shrugged, made sure I had everything I needed, and left the ballroom.

CHAPTER EIGHT

When I stepped from the ballroom, my intention was to find the staff and conduct interviews, just as Viola requested. I realized I had three issues to overcome with the task.

First, I didn't know who all the staff were. From earlier, I learned of at least ten servers, and Heather, the caterer, but I didn't know if there was anyone else. I should have asked for a list from Brantley of who else might be around. For all I guessed, Hawthorne dedicated one entire wing of the house to cooks, butlers, drivers, caretakers, or whoever else Hawthorne Harris had on staff.

My second problem occurred to me right after the first one did. That one was I didn't know where to find anyone except Heather, whom I assumed had returned to her food truck. What was I supposed to do? Wander the halls like a ghost until I ran into people?

My third issue was my biggest hurdle. I had no actual authority. I'm a musician, not a cop, so although I could request that people speak to me, they had the complete right to tell me to bug off. Granted, when I talked to fans, they were always more than willing to talk to me, and would do so for as long as I let them. The staff may have never heard of me, so chances were I couldn't use my fourth-tier celebrity status to coax conversation from them. Still, Viola asked for my help, so I wanted to help. Even if half the people I encountered wouldn't say a word, that was that many fewer people she'd have to interview later.

My initial priority was to locate people to talk to, so I backtracked through the rooms I'd actually been in to see if anyone was around. I hit pay dirt on my first stop when I entered the room I'd eaten dinner in. Around the massive table sat Heather and the service crew.

"Codi Cassidy, come in and join us! I promise not to spill anything on you. Well, I'll try not to, anyway," Heather said when she noticed me standing in the doorway like I was waiting for an invitation to join the party.

As I stepped into the room, Heather used her foot to push out the chair next to her, and I took that as a sign to sit down and join her. I set the notebook on the table and placed the pen on it.

"Would you like something to drink?" Heather asked. "Carolina, pass the bubbly."

Carolina, who sat three people from Heather, picked up the bottle before her without breaking the conversation with the person next to her. From there, I watched as the bottle transferred from hand to hand until Heather grabbed it. She held it up to the light to check how much volume remained, then topped off her glass.

"No, thank you. I'm not big on wine," I said.

"What's your pleasure, then? Whiskey, probably, or perhaps a beer? I can give you whatever you want."

"A bottle of water would be perfect," I said.

"Liz, throw a bottle of water down here, will you?" Heather yelled across the table.

I looked down to see which one was Liz and spotted her at the opposite end of the table. She reached down and came up with a bottle from somewhere beneath the table. I saw her raise it above her head, then before I might utter a word to stop it, Liz tossed it into the air. To her credit, Liz had a great arm and Heather caught it in midair without hesitation. She handed it to me without comment.

"That was impressive," I admitted as I opened the bottle and took a drink.

Heather laughed. "Not really. We're on a baseball team together. So, what's up, buttercup?"

I moved my chair close enough to Heather for our knees to touch, then leaned in.

"Did you hear about Hawthorne Harris?" I asked.

Heather turned her champagne flute in her fingers, then drained the glass without pausing.

"I did. We all did."

I didn't recall seeing either Heather or any of the service staff in the minutes leading up to the big event, but that meant nothing. Distracted by the performance, I might well have missed someone popping in and out.

"Is it true he's dead?" Heather asked as she refilled her flute.

"It's true." I paused for a moment to watch her drink, hoping I could catch any visual clues from her, but I didn't. "Do you have any information about it?"

"I don't have much to tell you. I was in my truck cleaning things up. Dinner was done, therefore, so was I."

"Why didn't you leave?" I asked, curious since I usually liked to bail out myself the second the contract obligation ended.

Heather tilted her glass toward the rest of the women at the table. As she did so, she spilled some drink over the glass's edge, and it plopped onto the table. She didn't seem to notice. I did, and since there was an unused napkin within reach, I dropped it over the mess. Instinctively, Heather took the napkin, wiped up the wine, and threw the napkin onto a used laundry pile near the wall. The pile was already tall with napkins, tablecloths, shirts, and cummerbunds.

"These ladies are in my employ for the evening. Every single one. They're some of my regular subcontractors I use for servers, bartenders, valets. Whatever is needed for a party human resource-wise, I usually provide. For a price, of course."

"Of course," I agreed.

"Anyway," Heather continued, "after they're done, I like to make sure they're fed, paid, and have a ride home."

The payment comment struck a chord that I needed to explore further.

"I received a rumor that Mr. Harris had a bad habit of not paying his bills. Did you get paid for tonight?" I thought about the cash I'd squirreled away into my safe and reminded myself to thank Loren later for the tip to get the money up front.

Heather emptied her glass. Was that the third or fourth she'd downed since I'd been in the room? I couldn't remember. She coaxed the last of the liquid from the bottle and collected another three-quarters of a glass. She drank, then smiled.

"Oh, yeah. I got paid. I ask for one hundred percent upfront. For Hawthorne Harris, I also included the costs of the people I brought with me. I inflated prices to boot since I knew the tightwad wouldn't tip anyone at the end of the night."

"And he was good with that arrangement?" I asked.

"He had to be. I'm the only caterer who'll work with him now, other than Loren, for the pies. Every contract I have for other clients is fifty percent up front, balance due the day of the event. The first time I worked with Harris, he conveniently forgot to pay the rest of the bill. He blamed it on a bookkeeping error, and although he said he'd get the money to me right away, it took me almost eight months to get paid."

"But he finally paid?" I asked.

"He had to. Summer rolled around and he was looking for a caterer for a picnic, and he called every caterer within a hundred-mile radius, and everyone was busy. Then my phone rang, and he agreed to not only to pay the back balance but also agreed to the new terms."

"It's a good thing for you then that everyone else was booked."

Heather laughed and waved away my comment. "Oh, posh. Any one of two dozen caterers had open calendars then. They simply didn't want to deal with his nonsense. It's not like I was the first one he screwed over, and we caterers do talk to each other."

"Were you alone in the truck while you were cleaning up? Can anyone vouch for you?" I asked.

"You're asking me for an alibi?" Heather responded.

I could tell right then she was a straight shooter, so I returned the favor. "Yes."

"Liz," Heather yelled across the table. "Can you tell Codi here where I was over the last hour?"

Without hesitation, Liz answered. "On the truck, cleaning."

"How do you know?" Heather asked.

"Because I helped. Don't you remember me standing right beside you? Cut back on the booze, Heather," Liz answered.

A lady near the middle of the table raised her hand. I hadn't caught her name. "I can vouch for both of them. Thanks to drawing the short straw, I got to run equipment and food back and forth from the truck to inside."

There were eleven women at the table, and I had alibis for three of them. I looked from person to person at the table.

"You're wondering about the rest of them?" Heather asked.

I nodded. "Yes, I am."

"After they finished their duties, they were all in here, eating, drinking, making conversation."

"You're certain?" I asked.

"One hundred percent," Heather said.

"There's no one who slipped out of the room, then came back after someone killed Harris?"

"It's plausible, but doubtful."

"Why?" I asked.

"No motive. So far as I believe, no one in here has even talked to Hawthorne outside of their duties. And since I'm the one who pays them, there's no need for them to worry about anything except spilling soup on someone."

Heather made a convincing argument. Despite that, I needed to verify things for myself.

"Do you mind if I ask around? Take statements and contact information for the chief?" I asked out of politeness, since I was going to do it regardless of the answer.

"Be my guest," Heather said. "Listen up, everyone. Codi here is going to go around and ask you some questions. Please give her all the answers she needs and make them the truth."

The women at the table took in the advice, then went back to their conversations.

"They'll play ball. Do your thing."

"Thanks for your cooperation," I said.

I spent the next hour taking statements and photographs, and each story I gathered fit like a clean puzzle piece. Everyone collaborated on everyone else's whereabouts. Heather, Liz, and the other woman, who turned out to be named Malorie, all had airtight alibis.

In the end, I was no closer to getting any farther than I was before. When I finished taking the last statement, I returned to the seat next to Heather and reviewed all my notes to make sure my work didn't contain any major holes. Finally, I closed the notebook, and pushed it away from me.

"Well?" Heather asked.

"Well, I think your entire group is in the clear."

"Except Stacy and Ashley," Heather said.

"Who?" I asked.

"The bartenders. They should have been in the ballroom all night working at the bar."

I slapped myself on the forehead. "Ashley and Stacy."

I'd spoken with them both earlier in the evening, and remembered how helpful they'd been, then completely forgot about them.

"They're probably innocent, too," Heather said.

In my mind, I agreed, but I still needed to get statements from them, provided Viola hadn't already. "I'll have to talk to them. Can you think of anyone else, maybe someone from Hawthorne's staff, who might have been here tonight? Drivers, butlers, those sorts of people?"

Heather leaned back in her chair and considered the question for a moment. "You'd best ask that question to Brantley Wilson. Since he's Hawthorne's assistant, he would have the list. I assume there are gardeners on staff, as well as a regular chef and a driver, but I didn't see any of them around today. I don't know who else might work here, and it wouldn't surprise me if Harris had the same issue with other workers as he did hiring caterers. After all, there's no shortage of rich people around here who have yards to maintain and meals they need cooked. And they generally pay their people with a modicum of respect, unlike how I imagine the staff around here gets treated."

I wracked my brain for another question to ask when the gong sounded. Heather rolled her eyes.

"What?"

"It's that damn gong. Gets on my nerves every time. Is that the pinnacle of entitlement, or what? Does Hawthorne think he's a king or something?"

"Not anymore," I said. "Where does the gong come from? What sets it off?"

"I don't have the faintest. I imagined he had some button or something to push that rings it, but I'm not totally sure about that. All I know is when it sounds during dinner service, the next course should be served. Stupid gong. Do I look like one of Pavlov's dogs to you?"

Heather drained her glass, picked up the bottle, realized it was finally empty, and slammed it back down on the table. The bottle tipped over, rolled a few inches, and fell from the table. I heard the thump as it connected with the wood floor, but fortunately, it didn't break. Heather didn't move a muscle to check on it.

I decided I had all I needed from this group, so I excused myself and left the room.

Rather than return right away to the ballroom, I thought I'd explore the house a little. I made my way back to the home gym. Through the large windows, I saw the rain pelt the ground in fat drops and the lightning continued to strike as the storm continued. During a brief flash of light, I saw Heather's truck and my bus just beyond it, both sitting still in the rain. I hoped the kids were all okay. Since four out of five were technically wild animals, I suspected they fared fine. As a bit of thunder pealed, I pictured Gibson searching out a hiding spot on the bus, probably under my desk, or in my closet if I left the door open.

I left the gym, and instead of turning right, I walked straight ahead down a corridor. It wasn't a long corridor, but it certainly stretched farther than the length of my bus, and I thought, the length of most houses I'd been in.

The half-dozen doors before me were closed, but that didn't bother me since I knew how to solve that problem. I turned the knob of the first one I came to and pushed it open. I turned on the light and discovered I'd found a bathroom. It was only a half-bath, and had only a toilet and a sink, but it was still more impressive than most. To my surprise, the toilet was a standard porcelain one, and not made of solid gold like I expected. The pedestal sink appeared made of marble, and its fixtures were solid brass. There was a lone towel hanging on a rack, monogrammed with Hawthorne's initials. I rubbed a corner between my fingers and determined it was thicker and plusher than some carpets I've stood on.

I left the room and returned to the corridor. There, I crossed the hall and tried the door. Locked. I wandered up the hallway and found each door locked. I considered returning to the bus for my lock picks, but then I heard the peal of thunder, and I remembered the rain and elected to stay warm and dry in the house. Instead, I backtracked to where I'd come from and eventually made it back into the ballroom.

"How's it going in here?" I asked Laurel, who was sitting just inside the room where I'd left her.

"Well, no one else got shot in your absence, so I consider that a win," Laurel said.

I looked toward Bozeman's way. He was right where I'd left him, and it didn't look like he'd moved a muscle. "He's taking his job seriously," I said.

"He sure is. Although he did one of those jerk awake things about twenty minutes ago, looked around to see if anyone noticed, then went right back to his nap," Laurel said.

I smiled; sorry I had missed it. It was a classic Bozeman move that I'd experienced several times. The look on his face was always hilarious when he woke, not knowing where he was.

"What's Viola been up to?"

"She's been slowly making her way around the room. And I mean slowly. I think that's only the second person she's talked to since you left."

I scanned the room. Viola was currently talking to Danny Ewing. Everyone else was still clustered in small groups, and to my surprise, the bar was still open and serving drinks. I returned my attention to Laurel.

"Two people? I've been gone for over an hour."

"Yep. She talked to Brantley for most of that time. She's only been with that guy for about ten minutes now."

"How are you holding up?" I didn't need to ask, because I could tell simply by looking at Laurel that she was tired, stressed, and ready to leave.

"I'm good. A little bored, but I'm still hanging in there."

"You look exhausted," I said, perhaps a little more bluntly than I intended.

Laurel looked at me for a moment. "Okay, maybe I could use a quick nap. And perhaps a slice of Loren's pie."

The mention of the pie caused my stomach to growl. I wouldn't mind one myself.

"Why don't you take a break, and I'll check with Viola and see when we can get out of here."

"Thanks. I could use something to drink," Laurel said. She stood, stretched, and headed for the bar. I wanted to call after her and ask her to avoid alcohol, but she was an adult, so if she needed something to take the edge from a wayward night, she could have it.

From my spot, I watched as Viola talked to Danny, and I waited. I didn't want to interrupt since it wasn't like we were at a cocktail party, and I wanted to insert myself into a conversation. As I watched, I noticed the conversation must have taken an unexpected turn. Danny started flailing his arms around and now looked like a monster trying to fend off a swarm of wasps. In response, Viola took three steps backward to give him room.

"What do you think is going on there?" Laurel asked as she handed me a glass.

I was so intent on watching Viola and Danny, I never sensed Laurel's return, and I accepted the glass and drank without even checking the contents. I drained the Diet Coke from the glass and placed the empty vessel on the nearest table. To Laurel's credit, it was without a hint of alcohol.

"You're thinking of going over there, aren't you?" Laurel asked.

I passed Laurel a glance that should have said everything that needed to be said, but I answered. "Of course. What's the worst that could happen?"

Laurel winced. "I hate it when you ask that question."

CHAPTER NINE

I waited for a few seconds more, then finally, Viola dismissed Danny. While Danny walked toward the bar, Viola dipped her head and reviewed the notes she'd taken. The thunder rumbled; the lights flickered. My eyes instinctively focused on the chandelier overhead, as did Viola's. When I brought my gaze back down, I caught sight of Viola as she dropped the pen she held. As she bent to pick it up, once again, the lights dropped out, and darkness shrouded the room. I expected them to come back on within a few seconds, but they didn't.

Around me, the silence broke as a few murmurs erupted, and as the lights failed to come on, I heard an uncomfortable laugh. A moment later, I caught a sound that didn't belong, like someone had dropped a Santa sack filled with laundry onto a table. Fifteen seconds later, the lights returned, and I noticed right away I had another problem to contend with.

"Viola!" I screamed as I rushed toward her. She was lying on the floor on her side, her back to me. Next to her prone body was one of the giant candlesticks from a side table. Even with a cursory glance, I noticed the fresh blood along the bottom edge.

I dropped on my knees next to Viola and reached for her neck.

"Thank goodness," I said as I detected a pulse. I moved my hand from her neck to her chest and felt it rise. Viola and I both exhaled at the same time.

"What happened?" Laurel asked as she kneeled beside me.

"Whacked in the head," I answered.

I leaned over Viola's body, intending to turn her onto her back.

"Wait, stop," Laurel said.

I froze while Laurel did the same things I did, checking Viola's pulse and then her breathing.

"Leave her the way it is. You there, get something I can put under her head, and get me some water and a compress."

I thought Laurel was giving me directions, but when I looked up, I spotted Helen Troy rushing away.

"What do you want me to do?" I asked.

"Nothing, I got this."

I stayed out of the way as Laurel checked Viola's pulse again, then moved her top arm farther out, like Viola was reaching for something in front of her body.

"I don't want her to throw up and choke," she explained.

We waited another minute, and Helen returned carrying a bottle of water, a napkin, and a tablecloth.

Laurel opened the bottle, dumped some on the napkin, and checked out Viola's wound.

"You still have my phone?" she asked.

Without a word, I handed it over. Laurel took it, turned on the flashlight, and pointed it at Viola's head. "Hold it right there."

I did as I was told and watched as Laurel dabbed at the wound. "I don't think this is too bad. It looks like it already stopped bleeding, but I'm going to apply some pressure to make sure."

"Is she going to be okay?" I asked.

"Beats me. I'm a fiddle player, not an EMT."

"Where'd you learn to do this? Girl Scouts? Medical training?" I asked, genuinely curious.

Laurel smiled. "Mostly television." She removed the napkin from Viola's head and showed it to me. Even with my limited experience, I could tell the wound wasn't serious.

"When she wakes up, I imagine she's going to have one nasty headache. And hopefully not a severe concussion."

"Can you keep an eye on her?" I asked.

"Certainly," Laurel responded without hesitation.

Satisfied Viola would come through fine, I stood. Around me, I studied the faces of the rest of the people in the room, every eye following every move I made. My eyes dropped to the floor and saw Viola's pen laying on the ornate Italian marble. I picked it up and did a quick search until I spotted the corner of the cover of the notebook she'd been using under her right heel. With care, I lifted her leg, pulled out the book, and gently set her back down.

I righted myself and looked around. Brantley Wilson had moved to within two feet of me. His hat was askew, as was his quiver, and his left knee, bony and pale, had broken through his tights. Instead of saying anything, he stood staring at me, and after a moment, his foot started tapping out a Morse code message I couldn't decipher. Eventually, my impatience got the best of me.

"What?" I asked.

Brantley put his hands on his hips and leaned forward, nose turned slightly upward. "What are you going to do?"

The question confused me. "About?"

His right hand broke free, and he swirled his hand at Viola, and then in the general direction of Hawthorne's covered body. "All this. What do you intend to do about all this?"

"I don't really understand."

"I know you were helping her, so now what?"

"You don't get it. She only wanted me to take names and pictures of the staff, so she didn't miss anyone. I'm not a police officer, I'm a musician. You saw me up there doing my thing, didn't you?" I pointed toward the stage for effect.

"But you seem to have experience with what you're doing. Keep doing it."

I turned and discovered the speaker was the woman dressed as Dorothy, whose name I had already forgotten. Somewhere she'd misplaced her basket, so I imagined she lost poor Toto somewhere.

"Look, um, Dorothy, I don't know what you've learned, but there's nothing I can do here."

It was Loren's turn, so he stepped forward and spoke. "Bozeman told me the story about how you got him out of a bunch of trouble. He's told me you've solved mysteries before."

"It's not like that. This is a police matter, not mine. I'm sure backup is already on the way and will be here in no time."

Brantley shook his head. "How? No one got a call out. There's no reason for anyone in the outside world to speculate that anything out of the ordinary has gone on here tonight."

"I hate to jump in, Codi, but you're also missing the bigger picture."

That voice I recognized. A quick turn of my head verified that Bozeman had not only woken from his nap but had placed his feet firmly on the floor and tipped his hat back. He didn't speak much, but when he did, he commanded attention.

I sighed. "What's that, Boze?"

Bozeman lifted his arm and swept his finger across everyone in the room. "One of these fine people here is a murderer. Almost two-times over, I reckon."

I followed the direction of Bozeman's finger as he did another pass. As I did, I looked each person in the eyes. Then I glanced over at Laurel, who still tended to Viola, and across the room at the shrouded body. Bozeman was right. Someone had not only killed, but attempted to do so a second time. If the power remained shaky all night, chances are there might be more prone bodies on the ballroom floor.

At last, I relented. "Okay. I'll do it. I'll keep looking into this. With conditions."

"Okay. Name them," Brantley said.

"First. No one leaves or enters this room. Everyone finds a seat and stays put."

"What about the restroom? I need to go now, in fact," Frankenstein's bride said. I'd forgotten her name too, although I was confident it began with an A. Annie, maybe.

She had a good point, so I considered the question for a moment. "Okay. Bathroom breaks excepted, but only one person at a time, and with an escort. Either myself, Laurel, or Bozeman will take you to the bathroom and back."

"How do we know you weren't involved?" Danny stepped forward and asked.

To my surprise, Loren fielded the question for me. "Come on, man. You really think that when the lights darkened, one of those musicians, who have met none of you before, put down their instrument, crept across the room in the dark, killed Hawthorne Harris, and then took their place back on stage?"

Danny's shoulders slumped, followed by his eyes. "Okay, yeah. That seems improbable."

"More like impossible," Helen interjected.

"Okay, escorts to the bathroom," Brantley said. "What else?"

"No more alcohol comes out of the bar tonight. Only sodas and water from here on out. Coffee, if they have it."

Danny raised his glass and was about to protest when Loren wagged a finger at him in a distinctive no gesture. Danny closed his mouth and set his empty glass on the ground.

"Done," Brantley said. "And?"

"And everyone stays seated and cooperates. No one refuses to answer my questions."

"What is all this really going to buy us?" Dracula asked.

One of my first points of business needed to be relearning everyone's name.

Brantley turned. "Maybe she'll be able to finger the perpetrator. Is that not good enough?"

"So what?" Dracula's fake fangs impeded his speech, so he ripped them from his mouth and tossed them on the floor. "So what?" he repeated. "It's not like anything she gets will be admissible in court, even if she figures out who did it."

Loren stepped forward. "The benefit is, Claude, if she figures it out, we can hold that person for the authorities so no one else ends up like Viola, or worse, Harris."

I don't know if it was Loren's logic or his impressive size that convinced Claude the vampire to back down, but he did.

"Anything else?" Brantley asked.

I didn't think of anything at the moment. "That's it for now. Why doesn't everyone grab a seat and get comfortable? I'm sure it's going to be a long night."

The crowd disbursed, and as a group, they wandered around until each one found a chair. Instead of conversations in small groups like before, everyone seemed fine to be on their own for the moment.

I took a few steps over to Bozeman.

"What's your plan?" he asked.

"I carry on where Viola left off. Talk to the group, see what I can figure out."

"What do you want me to do?"

"Start by escorting that one woman to the bathroom, and then watch my back for me."

Bozeman tipped his hat and stood. "You got it."

"Oh, and Bozeman? Don't get yourself killed."

Bozeman shot me a smile that told me not to worry, and he headed toward the bride.

I sat down in Bozeman's seat and opened the notebook. I expected it to be filled with names, descriptions, random thoughts, or other information I remembered seeing scribbled in my dad's books. Instead, the notebook was empty except for the first three pages. She'd filled the first page with swirls. I'd seen plenty of swirls like that in my lifetime since I created the same ones when I tested to see if a pen was out of ink.

The second page didn't contain swirls, but rather squares. I almost pictured the design being made. A large square placed in the center, then two lines dividing it into fourths. Then she'd added more and more squares until it grew to the size of a chessboard, and then, for good measure, she'd penned in even more squares.

The third page, rather than the murderer's name written in bold letters in the center with arrows pointing to it, contained triangles. I could tell the page started off like the square page did, but she inked in diagonal lines to bisect the squares into triangles. Viola hadn't completely finished the project, as there were still several squares that were still squares.

"What in the world?" I whispered. "What was this all about?"

It tempted me to tear the pages from the book, but I thought that might give the wrong impression to anyone watching me. I flipped to the fourth page, grabbed my pens, and stood. I knew who I wanted to talk to first.

It didn't take me long to traverse the ballroom to the bar. Ashley was still manning her post, but Stacy was in a chair a few feet away, looking at something on her phone.

"Would you like a drink?" Ashley asked as I approached. "I can offer you a variety of soft drinks and water." She lowered her voice so only I could hear her. "I also have a pitcher of iced tea, but honestly, most of the ice in it has melted, so it's probably pretty diluted by now."

"I'll take a bottle of water," I said.

Ashley handed it over, and I opened the top and drank. I hadn't realized until that moment how thirsty I was. As I drank,

I gave Ashley the once over. Like the servers, she had flowing brown hair, clinched into a ponytail. Unlike the others, it suited her. I could easily picture that ponytail trailing through the back of a baseball cap as she biked or hiked the endless trails in the area. She tugged at the black vest she wore like it constricted her like a python. Even though she looked uncomfortable, she kept her professionalism.

"Lemme guess, you're here for information, not just the water, correct?" Ashley said as she picked up a bar rag and ran it over the top of the bar, even though I couldn't see a drop of liquid or stain upon it.

I took another swallow, then nodded. "Can I start by getting your full name, your phone number, and your picture?"

She smiled and asked for the notebook. I complied, and she took a pen from behind her ear, then jotted down her personal details in block letters which were easily readable. I appreciated that. Even with my own writing, I was often sloppy enough that I couldn't read my own notes. After I snapped her picture, I took the notebook back, added the date and time, and began.

"Where were you when everything happened?" I asked, getting right to the point.

"Right here."

"The entire night?"

"Yep."

"You didn't leave? Go to the bathroom? Run for supplies?"

Ashley smiled and shook her head. "Nope. Stacy is my runner, and I used the facilities before my shift started."

I didn't do the math, but it had been several hours since the night began.

"You haven't moved? You must have really comfortable shoes."

"It's all about the mat," Ashley said.

I was about to ask when she invited me behind the bar. There, underneath Ashley's feet, was a thick cushioned mat.

"That looks comfortable. You mind if I give it a try?" I asked.

Ashley moved aside, and I took her place behind the bar. Climbing onto the mat was like stepping onto a cloud.

"This is amazing," I admitted as I moved to my proper side of the bar.

"It is. Heather provided it for us. She's always watching out for our comfort. I can stand on this thing for an entire shift and not feel any worse for wear by the end of the night."

"If you didn't go anywhere, what did you see or hear?" I asked.

"A couple of the girls came around to serve the champagne at the beginning, and after that was gone, the guests started coming to me for drinks."

"Is it an open or cash bar?"

"Open, with limitations. Hawthorne Harris provided the alcohol I used tonight."

"He gave it to you himself?"

"No. His assistant did. But I can tell you it's not the good stuff."

"What do you mean?"

Ashley reached behind the bar and pulled out four bottles of liquor. She turned the labels so I could read them. Before me, were whiskey, vodka, cognac, and a rum bottle.

"See these? They are all top shelf all the way. This bottle of vodka would normally go for three hundred bucks. The rum, eighteen hundred. The others are also so top shelf I wouldn't be able to reach them."

"Okay, so he serves the best booze."

Ashley shook her head. "No. He doesn't. These bottles have been married."

She saw the look of confusion on my face and continued her explanation. She held up the whiskey bottle. "Someone has emptied this bottle of whiskey of the good stuff and replaced it with a brand us commoners would drink."

"You're sure?" I asked.

"Definitely. I've been tending bar a long time, and I know my booze."

"Has anyone else noticed?" I asked.

"If they did, no one has said anything about it."

"Has anyone drinking too much tonight?"

"Frankenstein has been by several times. If it wasn't a private party, I would have cut him off a long time ago."

"Has he been a problem?"

"Not as much as Dracula has."

"What do you mean?"

"He's only been over twice, but he was gross both times. The first time he asked for my number, the second he pinched Stacy on the bottom. What is it about men? Put them into capes and they turn into Neanderthals."

"I don't know the answer to that one, but it isn't just capes. It's also blue jeans, cowboy hats, boots, and a million other things. It probably all comes down to the drink, though."

Ashley nodded. "I'd agree with that."

"Have you noticed anything else out of the ordinary?"

"Not really. I've gone through more wine than anything. Most parties are like that."

"What about when the lights went out? Did you see anything or anyone?"

"No. The lights went out, gong sounded, lights came on, and you know what happened from there."

"You saw no one moving around? Anyone who might have approached Hawthorne, or even Viola?"

"No. I wish I could be more help. To be honest, I have horrible night vision, anyway. Once the lights grow dim, I can't see a thing."

I had no more questions for her, so I moved on to Stacy. As I got closer, I noticed she was still fiddling with her phone.

"Do you have a cell signal?" I asked.

Stacy looked up at me, back at her phone, then up at me. "Oh. No. I don't. I'm doing a crossword puzzle offline."

"Too bad. I was hoping you had contacted the outside world somehow."

Stacy turned off the phone and shoved it into her pocket. She, too, had long brown hair and wore the same tuxedo as Ashley, although her shirt tails had pulled free and peeked out beneath her vest. Over the course of the night, she'd worked up enough of a sweat to turn the shirt under her arms translucent. Now that I took a good look at her, she looked younger than all the other women I'd talked to that night.

Stacy confirmed my suspicions when she told me she was only nineteen. She had been busy all night running all over the place to keep the bar stocked with booze, beer, wine, and ice. I got Stacy's contact information and photo and asked her the same questions I'd asked Ashley. She gave me a detailed version of her encounter with Dracula, but other than that, she provided no more information than I'd gotten from Ashley.

Satisfied all of Heather's people were in the clear, it was time to turn my attention to the big fish in the room.

CHAPTER TEN

I tried to decide who to talk to first and that decision became easy for me when I spotted, of all people, the missing Jackie May. She was sitting alone in the far corner of the room, wedged between a wall and a window. I hadn't seen her come in and did not have a clue when she'd arrived. Clearly, my powers of perception were a bit off.

I headed right toward her. Once I got to within ten feet, I grabbed a chair and dragged it with me across the floor. I placed it right in front of Jackie and sat. I leaned forward, my expression a mix of concern and minor annoyance.

"Hey, Jackie. Where have you been?" I asked, my tone gentle.

She looked at me, but at first, I didn't think she recognized me, even though she was the reason I was here in the first place.

"Codi, I..." she trailed off. She'd learned what happened. Crying had turned her eyes red-rimmed, and her mascara had run, giving her the same look my pet raccoon generally had. She sat with her hands folded tightly in her lap, and she subconsciously fiddled with her engagement ring.

"Jackie? Can you hear me, honey?"

She blinked twice and sniffed. I looked around for a tissue, and not finding one, I gave up on the search.

"Where were you all night?" I waited.

After almost a full minute, tears welled up in Jackie's eyes, and she took a deep breath before responding. "You gave me that shirt, and I wanted to put it away so it wouldn't get ruined. I took it to my room. Hung it in my closet."

"That happened several hours ago. What happened next?" I asked.

Jackie stared at the floor for a bit. If her head were transparent, I probably would have been able to see the gears turning.

"Well, the storm. Lots of thunder and lightning. Then the power died. Hawthorne always said if the power died to go into the room and stay there until he came for me. I went in, but he never came. I fell asleep waiting, and when I woke up, he still wasn't with me, so I came back here."

"What room?"

"The room. There's a room in the back of Hawthorne's closet. It isn't big like his bedroom. There's only enough room for a small bed, one of those mini fridges, a microwave, and a bunch of computer monitors."

"Is there a thick door? With a lock of some sort?" I asked.

"How did you guess?" Jackie asked, amazed by my powers.

The answer was simple. I'd seen safe rooms in several movies and television shows.

"Are you okay if I ask you a few questions?" I asked.

Jackie nodded.

"Did anything unusual happen during dinner or afterward?" I asked.

Jackie shook her head. A strand of her hair fell from behind her ear and across her face. "No, nothing unusual. Just the typical dinner party chitchat. You were there, so I don't need to tell you how it happened."

"I wasn't there the entire time," I corrected. "I only stopped by for a quick meet and greet."

Jackie nodded. "That's right. I remember now."

"Did Hawthorne mention any conflicts or trouble with anyone at the party?"

Jackie hesitated, her gaze dropping to her hands. She seemed to fixate on the diamond on her finger, and as she touched the ring, she started to cry again. "No. He didn't have any problems with anyone here."

Based on my conversations with Heather and Loren's insistence that I get my cash in advance, I detected a lie, assuming she knew how Hawthorne did business.

"Okay. If everyone at the party was okay, did he ever mention any enemies? Anyone at all who might have wanted to harm him?" I asked.

Jackie's head shook back and forth. "No. Of course not. Everyone loved him. He got along with everyone. No one would want to hurt a single hair on his head."

Again, I imagined that was stretching the truth by a bit. I figured she didn't want to speak ill of the dead. Or perhaps she preferred to wear the rose-colored glasses that prevented her from thinking anything bad about him.

"Did he have any secrets? Anything he might have kept from you?"

"No! Of course not. We were open with each other. We trusted each other with our deepest secrets."

I had trouble believing that one as well, as I jotted down a few notes to keep everything straight.

"You say you took a nap in the safe room? Why? I assumed you were excited to see my show."

Jackie looked at me in the eyes, then rubbed her forehead. "I'm not sure. I remember walking all the way to my room. The lights dimmed, and I rushed to the room. Then, from out of nowhere, I felt really sleepy. I couldn't keep my eyes open. I think I fell asleep before I hit the pillow."

"And when you woke, you came right back here? You didn't go anywhere else?"

"That's right," she said.

"Did you see or talk to anyone in the hallway? Or when you got back here?"

She shook her head again. "No. When I got back here, I looked around for Hawthorne, and I knew that he was under there. I came here and haven't moved since."

Jackie took a moment, wiped away a tear and a good bit of mascara as well.

I looked around again for a tissue and spotted a napkin on a table nearby. Once I retrieved it, I handed it to Jackie, and she wiped her eyes and blew her nose.

"I realize this has been hard for you. If you can think of anything else, no matter how insignificant it may seem, let me know."

Jackie nodded, blew her nose again, and shut down.

I scanned the room, wondering who to talk to next, and decided on Brantley Wilson. In my mind, he was not only the most logical person to speak to as Hawthorne's assistant, but he was also the person physically closest to me. I reviewed my notes a final time, made one correction. Afterward, I made my way over to where Brantley was sitting at the edge of a table, one leg propped over the other, fingers drumming on the table. I slid into an empty chair next to him and placed the notebook on the table. I opened it to a blank page, added the date, time, and his name to the top. His gaze as he scrutinized me had an apprehensive expression on it.

"So, Brantley, how did you get that hole in your tights?" His eyes dipped from my notebook to his legs. He spotted the exposed knee. "I don't know. I think I must have run into something in the dark."

"It looks like you're bleeding there. You must have run into something sharp," I noted.

He bent at the waist and took a closer look. There, almost in the exact center of his patella, was a drop of blood. He licked his thumb and rubbed it away. As I watched, I noticed it came off cleanly. It didn't start bleeding again, and there didn't appear to be a spot of it left. I concluded the blood wasn't his. I also realized I made a mistake by pointing it out. Since he removed it, that evidence was now gone.

"Did you notice anything strange tonight?" I asked.

"You mean other than the two bodies lying on the floor?" he asked, with a side of snark.

I nodded.

"Not really. Just another Hawthorne Harris party."

"What's that mean?"

Before he could answer, the large feather on his felt cap drooped right over his eyes. In a flourish, he removed the hat and tossed it on the table. "He loved having these parties once or twice a month. Bring in his friends. Show off."

"You didn't seem to enjoy yourself tonight," I noted.

"That's because I was on the clock. You don't think he organized these things himself, do you? Nope. That's me. I have to take care of everything. Catering, entertainment, menu, seating arrangements. Everything. It's a hassle to do all that on top of my day job."

"What is your day job?" I asked.

"Anything Hawthorne tells me to do." Brantley took a moment and glanced across the room at the body on the floor. "Told me to do. Correspondence, post office runs, meeting setups, driving. Anything and everything."

"It sounds like he trusted and relied on you."

Brantley scoffed. "Trusted? Right. He didn't trust anyone. No one."

"What about her?" I asked, pointing my pen in Jackie's

direction. "Did he trust her?"

Brantley's brow furrowed, and he shifted uncomfortably in his seat. He leaned in closer and lowered his voice. "Not her, either."

That surprised me. "Then why would they get married?"

Brantley shrugged. "I don't think he ever intended on actually marrying her. After they got together, she was always pushing for that rock on her hand, and ever since, she's been pushing him to set a date for the wedding. He's been avoiding that topic for months."

"Why would he keep her around?" I asked.

"Eye candy. Nothing more. Older man of his status is always looking for a beautiful woman to hang around. To him, she was a symbol, like the Bentley in the garage."

I wanted to direct the conversation in a direction away from Jackie. "How's the pay?"

Brantley's hesitation to answer was clear. He grabbed his hat and fiddled with the feather, like a preening bird. "It's fine."

"Did you get paid on time?" I asked.

I could tell he didn't like the question, because he didn't answer.

"You agreed to cooperate with me, Brantley. Come on. Did you get paid?"

After a long pause, he answered. "Eventually."

I made a few notes in the book.

"Did Mr. Harris mention anything concerning, or out of the ordinary recently? Get any threats? Any hate mails?" I asked.

Brantley smiled. "Any rocks with notes attached thrown through the window? Mr. Harris is… was a powerful, rich man. People were always giving him threats of lawsuits, or threats against his person. Especially the environmentalists. We hear from different groups at least six times a week blathering on about over-fishing and saving the planet and whatever."

"Did he have any enemies?" I asked.

"He's put more than a few people out of business as he's consolidated operations in the area, so probably. I don't have any names in my head offhand, but I'm sure I could get you a list."

"Is there anyone here who'd like to do him any harm?"

Brantley took a moment to scan the room. Based on his demeanor, I sensed his reluctance to divulge more information. He seemed to hold something back, but he didn't say. Finally, his eyes came back to mine. "You'd have to ask them."

I wrote a few more notes, then thanked Brantley and left him alone. Thirsty again, I returned to the bar and got another bottle of water from Ashley. I still had another half-dozen people to talk to, and as I drank, I considered who to approach next. Then I caught the echoing clack of ruby slippers against the marble floor and noticed Dorothy headed my way. She stopped at the bar, asked for a Diet Coke, and once she had a glass in hand, she stepped toward me.

"What's up, buttercup?" she asked.

"Can we talk?" I asked.

"That's why I came over. I'd like to get the interrogation over with."

I laughed. "It's hardly an interrogation. Just a few questions. Let's have a seat."

Dorothy followed me to the nearest table, and we sat. I turned the page in the notebook and added the date and time to the top of the page and asked for her full name.

"Amelia, with an A. Last name Brown, like the color."

As I took down the name, Amelia adjusted the blue gingham dress she was wearing. The light from the chandelier reflected off the sequins sewn into the fabric. As she waited for questions from me, she fidgeted with the hem of her skirt, then folded her hands on top of the table.

"Can you tell me how you knew Hawthorne?"

Amelia took a drink before she answered. "I'm his chief accountant. He's been a client of mine for several years."

"Is it true he had trouble with paying people?" I blurted out. Not where I wanted to start, but I couldn't stop now.

As Amelia stared at me, I noticed one of her irises was a deeper brown shade than the other.

"He paid all his bills within the limits of accepted accounting principles," she said.

That was the longest yes or no answer I'd ever gotten to a question. "What does that mean?"

"That means he paid all his bills within the limits of accepted accounting principles."

My inside voice screamed at dippy Dorothy that repeating the same answer word for word didn't provide any additional context. My outside persona smiled and recorded the quote verbatim.

"Did he pay you on time?" I hoped a simple question would generate an equally similar answer.

"Yes." Amelia crossed her arms and sat back in her chair. She started to pull away from me, and I'd barely begun the questioning.

"Did you witness anything when the murder occurred?"

"The lights went out, that gong sounded, and that was all I can tell you."

"Who were you near at the time?"

Amelia didn't answer right away, but I can tell she was working on coming up with one. "Danny Ewing? I don't know for sure, but he's been chatting me up all night. I can't shake the guy. Oh, and Claude. He's been equally creepy. Keeps saying he wants to suck my blood or some such nonsense. Apparently, he really got into character."

"Did Hawthorne get along with everyone here?"

Amelia shrugged. "I guess. They were all invited to the party, right? And everyone showed up rather than make other plans."

I leaned in a little closer. "Did Hawthorne ever mention

anything unusual or seem concerned about someone or something?"

Amelia's brow furrowed, and she tapped her chin thoughtfully. "Not to me, he didn't. You should ask Jackie or Brantley that question."

"Did he have any enemies or conflicts that you were aware of?"

Amelia shook her head. "Not that I know of. From my perspective, his business dealings were usually…smooth."

I smiled. "And he paid all of his bills on time?"

I got no response.

"Within the limits of accepted accounting principles?" I added.

Amelia hesitated for a second, then smiled and nodded. "That's right."

"What happens with you now that your biggest client is gone?"

Amelia smiled a half-smile. "He wasn't my only client. I'll be fine. And someone will have to take over his estate, and of course, they may choose to keep me on as their accountant."

Her comment sparked a thought, so on my pad I scratched down two words in block letters. I drew three boxes around the words and set the pen down.

"Is anyone else here your client?"

Although her words hesitated, I followed her eyes and her gaze passed beyond me to the crowd behind. I imagined she balanced somewhere between the truth and a lie and didn't want to answer the question.

Finally, she answered. "I'm not sure that question has anything to do with the incident. I doubt it would make a difference one way or another if someone here was a client of mine or not, and professional ethics wouldn't allow me to say, anyway."

"You're not going to say?"

"No." The word spoken with a hint of harshness to it.

"I was told I would have everyone's cooperation if I agreed

to do this," I said.

Amelia spotted a stray speck of lint on her dress, just above her left breast. She picked at it indifferently at first, then actively worked at setting it free. At last, she pulled the offending element from her, held it in the air for a moment to get a closer look at it, then let it fall to the floor. We both watched the white fuzz as it descended to the ground like a December snowflake.

"That was Brantley's deal, not mine," she said. "I'll answer any questions regarding tonight you may have, but I've got no interest in telling you about my business dealings or personal life unrelated to what happened here."

"Fair enough," I agreed. "Can you tell me anything about the attack on Viola Park?"

That question Amelia answered right away. "No more than I can tell you about the attack on Hawthorne. I saw you just before it happened, and since I can't see in the dark, I doubt I got any more knowledge about it than you do."

I couldn't dispute that. Whoever attacked Viola and Hawthorne had set it up perfectly to correspond with the cuts to the power. I made a note of that and hoped Brantley could shed a little light on it. Pun intended.

"Do you remember seeing Jackie come back into the room?"

Again, there was an extended pause, but I didn't think this one was one of evasion, but more one of recall.

"If I'm not mistaken, I was chatting with Loren at the time. Do you know him? Dressed as King Arthur? He's the pie king of central California. As we talked, I noticed Jackie staggering into the room. She looked around, probably for Hawthorne, and then she spotted the body on the floor. She stepped toward it, then walked backward until she fell right into the chair she's been sitting in since she got back."

"Do you know what time that was?"

"I can't tell you. I don't have a watch, and my phone is in my picnic basket."

When I glanced at her feet, I noticed she still didn't have it with her. "Where is it?"

Amelia shrugged. "If you have time for another mystery, I'd appreciate it if you solved that problem for me. You need anything else from me?"

I said no, and Amelia rose without fanfare, and after a stop at the bar for a Diet Coke refill, she returned to the group at the far end of the ballroom. I still had a few people to talk to, and as I moved to stand, I glanced back at the words I'd written earlier. A question that I needed to answer. Who inherits?

CHAPTER ELEVEN

The next person I wanted to talk to was Loren, and I spotted him easily because he stood out in the crowd. He was facing away from me and seemed deep in conversation with Bozeman. When I had been in the room earlier, I had bypassed him at the meet and greet because we'd already broken bread, or rather, pie, together. As I stepped closer, I marveled at how detailed his costume was. From the back, the first thing I noticed was his rich, velvet cloak attached to his broad shoulders. The cloak bore images of heraldry, and contained the emblematic dragon of Camelot, its scales shimmering with shades of gold. A ruby made up its eye.

Atop his head sat a well-crafted crown, adorned with glass jewels that caught the light and cast a kaleidoscopic effect around him.

I stepped up and stood off to the side, so not to interrupt Bozeman in mid-sentence.

"So that's when Sonny turned to me and said I should have warned him there was a quilting bee going on," Bozeman said.

I didn't see the humor in it since I'd missed most of the story, but Bozeman and Loren seemed amused by it. They both laughed, Bozeman so hard he let a snort loose that made me giggle.

"Aw, man, that's great. Whatever happened to old Sonny?" Loren asked as he regained his composure.

"Last I learned, his wife left with the kids, and he started hanging with the wrong people. Ended up in the state penitentiary. That was about ten years ago," Bozeman said.

"That's too bad. He had everything going for him. Goes to show that you just never know. You looking for me?"

I didn't realize Loren had addressed me, so I missed the question at first. It took me a moment to catch up.

"Sure. Do you mind if I pry you away for a minute or two?" I asked.

"Lead me away, my dear."

Loren turned toward me, giving me a full view of the rest of his costume. He wore a leather belt, embellished with intricate designs and fastened with a gleaming brass buckle. The belt held a scabbard that housed a sword. I had no doubt it was a replica of Excalibur. Although the scabbard covered the blade, I appreciated the mythical patterns that adorned the hilt.

When I first met Loren at the diner, he seemed like a giant, and the King Arthur getup made him even more imposing. As we walked to a nearby table, he carried himself as if he was the embodiment of the storied hero. Chivalry wasn't dead, as he waited to sit until I did.

"What can I do for you, milady?" Loren asked.

I smiled at him. "You can start by calling me Codi, and not milady."

Loren took the crown from his head and set it on the table. "Sorry. Sometimes I get too wrapped up in the role when I dress up."

"You do this often? Do you play King Arthur at the Renaissance fair?"

He smiled. I liked him and hoped he wasn't a murderer.

"No. But I do perform in the local theater productions when I can, and every December I always dress up like Santa and visit the local schools and shelters."

I could picture him dressed in a Santa suit. Because of his massive size and appearance, I wondered how many yuletide nightmares he gave children.

"What would you like to know, Codi?" Loren asked as he clasped his hands, threw one massive leg over the other, and leaned back in his chair.

"Anything you can tell me about tonight? Let's start with anything you know about the murder."

"I'm afraid I can't be much help there, Codi. Everything faded to black, and when the lights came back, I was just as shocked and surprised as anyone to see Hawthorne like that."

That answer seemed to be the outright winner, and to be honest, if someone asked me, it would be my reply as well. But I needed to ask that same question to everyone on the off chance someone noticed even the smallest of details.

"When the lights failed, you didn't see anything. That I get. I didn't either. Did you overhear anything? Like shoes squeaking on the floor? Or smell anything, like a passing cologne or perfume? Or sense anything, like a slight breeze as someone passed you?"

I hated the leading questions, but I'd gotten nowhere with the open-ended ones.

Loren dipped into silence. I couldn't hear him breathing, but I watched as his chest rhythmically rose and fell.

"No. Nothing. The only thing I got was a jab in the ribs."

"Where did that come from?"

Loren smiled. "From Viola. When the lights first dropped out, she got startled. She elbowed me right in the ribs."

"And you're sure it was her?"

He nodded. "Yep. She whispered an apology to me right after she hit me. Not that she needed to. I barely felt it."

"She whispered in your ear?"

Loren smiled. "More like in my upper arm. But it was her voice."

"Does anyone here have a problem with Hawthorne?" I asked.

Loren made a raspberry with his lips, then rolled his eyes. "Would be shorter if I told you who didn't."

"Okay, we can run with that."

"Did you get your money for tonight like I suggested?"

I nodded.

"So, then. You. Everyone else, excluding me and Viola, I'd be suspicious of," Loren said.

"Why should I let you off the list?" I asked.

"Remember how we talked in the diner? When he buys the pies, I have my system to get the bread. As long as he shoots straight with me, I got no problem with him."

"And why not Viola?"

Loren didn't answer. He pointed to where Viola lay still on the floor, Laurel still by her side.

"I doubt that she'd shoot Hawthorne in a room full of witnesses and then knock herself out to throw everyone off the scent," Loren said.

He had a valid point.

"What about when Viola got hit? Did you witness anything, then?"

I saw a flash of anger run through Loren's eyes. Then, just as quick, it transformed into a tinge of sadness.

"Again, I didn't see anything. But I can tell you that when I figure out who did it, that man is done."

I reached out and put my hand over his. "I'm sorry. Were you and Viola dating?"

Loren nodded. "We've been seeing each other on and off since she first moved here. It didn't mean to start out romantic, but…"

Loren trailed off, and I nodded. I understood since I've written more than my fair share of songs about friends that have become more over the passage of time. I felt the overwhelming need to change the subject.

"Tell me, are you a client of Amelia Brown?"

Loren leaned in and as he did, his shadow passed over me like a solar eclipse. "Did she tell you I was?" he whispered.

"No, but she eluded someone here is. Since you're a business owner, you are the most logical person."

Loren shook his head furiously. I suspected the crown would have flown from his head had it not been already on the table.

"Do not trust that woman," he growled. "I have it on good authority that she's a cheat and encourages her clients to cheat. And not only on their taxes."

"Has she ever approached you to be a client?"

"Oh, yes. She came to the diner once. All flash and no substance. Tried to talk her way right into being a business partner."

"What happened?" I asked.

"I tossed her out without fanfare and banned her from the place."

"If you're not working with her, does anyone here?"

Loren stood, turned, and started reviewing faces. As he did, he pointed at people, which told me that subtlety wasn't his strong suit. After a minute, he sat down again. "Maybe the Ewings. Maybe Claude. Hawthorne was for sure, but anyone else is simply a guess on my part."

"Based on what you told me before, you think everyone besides you and I potentially have a grievance with Hawthorne?"

Loren smiled. "I'd probably rule out Bozeman too. He wouldn't hurt a fly. Unless it was drunk and obnoxious. Oh, and the fiddle girl."

"Laurel," I provided.

"Right. Laurel."

"Why?" It was meant to be an internal question, but it slipped out.

"Money, sweetheart. The answer is always money. You think Jackie over there is attracted to a man almost three times her age because they have great conversations? Amelia's been cooking his books for years. Brantley's been the inside man for forever. Claude's his attorney. Money connects everyone here. It makes the world go around."

"What about the Ewings?" I asked. "Or Helen?"

"Good question. I've never met them before."

"Sorry. I just assumed you did," I said.

"I would have made the same mistake. But I would bet that the reason they're here is so Hawthorne could get something out of them."

I sighed. "Okay, I guess you can go on back to Bozeman.   I know where to find you if I need additional information."

Loren stood, put his crown back on his head, and bowed at me. "Yes, milady."

I laughed, and Loren walked away.

Since I had a moment alone, I took a few notes about things Loren had said, then quickly reviewed them. I looked around at who to talk to next. By my count, I was down to only four, and the first of those headed my way.

"Mind if I sit down?" Helen asked, taking the chair before I responded.

"Go ahead," I said.

"I noticed you standing alone over here and thought I'd come over instead of waiting for you to come to me. You were intending on coming to me, right?"

"Yep. Just about to come to you, in fact," I said, although I hadn't actually decided on who to pester next.

"I saw nothing happen. It was dark. Too dark. You remember, right? Boom! Lights gone out."

Helen was a bundle of energy, which, to me, didn't match the mood of everyone else in the room. Circumstances had trapped us in here together. Over several hours, with nothing to do except make awkward conversations with people we'd love to get away from, anyway. Not to mention the emotional drain of being witness to a murder and an assault.

"What about when Viola got attacked? Did you notice anything at all?" I asked.

Helen took a deep breath, like she was preparing to fill a balloon. "Nope. No. Not a single thing. Again. Lights out, lights on."

She stopped speaking, and I hesitated to ask another question. She seemed wired to me. I'd been around the music scene long enough to know when people were doing special substances. Although I'd always been clean, and expected Bozeman to remain the same, I'd seen enough people in a manic state like the one Helen currently displayed.

I hoped to tune down the volume a little and calm the situation.

"So, Helen, what do you do?"

"Do?" she asked.

"Yes. Like for work." I didn't think it was a hard question, but apparently, I was wrong.

"I'm..."

Helen trailed off like she'd fallen asleep, but she wasn't. Her eyes were wide open and darting back and forth, unable to focus on anything.

"Helen? Hello? Can you hear me?" I asked.

Whatever vacation she just went on ended, and her eyes settled back to mine.

"What do you do for work?" I repeated.

"I'm a personal trainer. Diet and fitness coach," she finally said.

In my mind, that would explain her excellent figure. Well, working out and the drugs I imagined she was on.

"Was Hawthorne one of your clients?" I asked.

She grinned. "Oh, yes. We had sessions almost every day. He was insistent about it. Said he wanted to pay… special attention to his physical fitness."

I felt the urge to give up an eye roll, but I fought it and won.

"Did he pay you?"

Her grin grew wider. "Oh, yes. He paid me very well."

"Did you work out with Jackie, too, or just Hawthorne?"

Her smile disappeared like I'd erased her face.

"No. Never her. Just him."

"And when everything went down tonight, you didn't notice something unusual?" I clarified.

"Nope," Helen answered.

"You didn't hear or smell anything?"

"Nope. Not a single thing. Can I go now? I need to use the restroom again."

"Again? How many times have you gone?"

Helen shrugged. "I don't know. You'd have to ask the cowboy." The right strap of her dress fell off her shoulder. She made a half-hearted attempt to fix it, but when it fell again, she gave up on the exercise.

I gathered up the notebook, wrapped my arm around Helen's, and led her away from the table.

When we got to within four feet of Bozeman, she pulled away from me and raced to him.

"Hey, cowboy. Can you escort me to the restroom?" Helen cooed.

"I can take you," I offered.

She waved me off. "Oh, no, that's fine. He knows the way. Don't you, cowboy?"

Bozeman exhaled through his nose, which was a telltale sign she irritated him. "Yes, ma'am. It's no trouble at all."

Bozeman got to his feet and Helen slipped under his arm like they were long-time lovers. Together, they walked off into the proverbial sunset, leaving Loren and me behind.

"She's an interesting one," I said.

"No doubt. She's bad news," Loren said.

I turned to face him. "Wait. I thought you said you've never met her."

"And that's true. But I know of her. She's been in the diner a few times. Usually trying to drum up business for whatever it is she's doing. What was it? Some kind of gym thing?"

"She told me she does personal training. Diet and fitness."

Loren scoffed. "Well, my staff tells me she likes to drum up other business. Usually down at the beach when the surfers come to town. I understand she likes to peddle the white powder, and I'm not talking about confectioner's sugar. You catch that drift?"

I nodded. "That would certainly explain her odd behavior. How many times has she gone to the bathroom?"
Loren scratched his chin. "I think three since Boze and I have been talking. Although I'm not sure if she's been using that as an excuse to talk to your man."

I considered the point for a second. Helen wouldn't be the

first woman who tried to get Bozeman's attention. There were plenty of times where after gigs we'd find a woman hanging around the bus waiting for him. One time, an entire bridal party had approached him. They hoped the cowboy would wrangle the bride into one last rodeo before she walked down the aisle the next morning. He never took anyone up on their kind offers. At least on the bus. If Bozeman was interested in a woman, he'd typically make sure his business happened away from the bus. I think that was partially out of respect for me, and partially out of his desire to keep his private life private.

"It's not my business, but I don't think she's really his type if she is trying to get some action," Loren said.

I remembered back to all the women I'd seen Bozeman take an interest in. He'd dated blonds, brunettes, and redheads. Tall women and short, skinny and heavier set. The thing that attracted him the most was personality, a good sense of humor, and sobriety.

"I agree. She's got no shot if she's playing that game."

"Did you get any information out of her?" Loren asked.

If I had him on the top of my suspect list, I would have avoided the question, assuming he was trying to get me off his trail, but at this point, I had other people in mind, so I took his question merely as a way to make small talk.

I shook my head. "Not really. In the condition she's in, I'm surprised she didn't answer a question about what her name is with a recipe for a peanut butter and jelly sandwich. One missing the jelly. And bread. And peanut butter. She was pretty much useless to me. I'll have to pass her back to Viola when she wakes up."

At the mention of Viola, Loren looked over to where she still lay quietly on the floor. I looked as well. Laurel was no longer sitting on the floor with her, but she had pulled a chair close and settled into it. She'd also taken the time to cover Viola with a folded over tablecloth. Although I wanted Viola to jump up and take control of the room, it pleased me to see Laurel was taking good care of her.

"Don't worry. She'll be okay," I said.

"How can you tell for sure?" Loren asked.

"Look at Laurel's face. Does she look worried?"

Loren's eyes went from the floor to Laurel. In silence, he studied her countenance for almost a full minute. "No. She looks tired and bored. And uncomfortable from sitting in that chair. But she doesn't look worried."

I put my hand on his shoulder. "Then you shouldn't either. Trust me. Viola will be fine."

"They're coming back," Loren said.

I shifted in my seat and watched as Bozeman escorted Helen into the room. Rather than bring her back in our direction, Bozeman guided her to the opposite side of the room and sat her down in a chair near where Amelia and Brantley were deep in conversation. Once he got her settled, Bozeman came back to us and took his seat. He removed his hat, put it on his lap, and ran his fingers through his hair.

"I reckon she needs some serious help."

"And let me guess, you're just the man to give it to her?" I prodded.

Bozeman, rather than speak, growled at me.

I smiled. "I take it no wedding bells are on the horizon then."

CHAPTER TWELVE

"Hi there," I said as I slid into the chair next to Danny Ewing. From somewhere he'd appropriated not one or two, but three bottles of wine.

Initially, he'd had the bottles of Sauvignon Blanc clustered in a little triangle, but one had tipped over at one point. Part of me wanted to pick it up and place it back where it belonged, complete with the labels lined up to the front, but I let the bottle lie where it was.

He stared at me for a moment before answering. I noticed the synapses were slow to fire, I suspected, because of the wine and whatever else he'd imbibed during the night. Finally, he found his focus.

"You're the band," he slurred.

"Part of it, anyway. What's your name?" I asked.

He smiled and sat straighter in his chair. I suspected he thought I was hitting on him. If that made him more willing to answer my questions, I was all for it.

"Danny. Danny Ewing."

"You're here with your wife, right?" I asked.

At the mention of the wife, Danny got a little rattled, and his eyes began to dart around the room, and he almost fell from his chair when he shifted to peek behind him.

"You see her anywhere?" he asked.

"Nope," I lied. She was sitting fifteen feet away and staring at me. I passed her a tentative wave. She waved back, but with only one finger. I was looking forward to my conversation with her.

"So, sugar, what's your phone number?"

He grinned like a jack-o'-lantern as he leaned toward me and told me the digits. He teetered for a moment, and I imagined gravity would eventually take hold and he'd tumble into my lap. I reached out for his shoulder and pushed him back into his chair.

"Do you like me? I look good, don't I?" he asked.

I stopped for a moment to glance at him.

On his feet, he wore square-toed platformed boots I suspected added a good three inches to his height. He wore a tattered, dark-colored suit, stitched together with different fabrics. Large, oversized patches adorned the clothing, creating a patchwork effect that reminded me of the creature's pieced-together appearance.

On his head, he wore a flat-topped wig of dark hair, but over the course of the night it had become dislodged and sat atop his dome at a slight angle like he was wearing a jaunty hat instead of a wig. I fought another urge, this one from ripping the thing from his head completely and tossing it across the room.

On the right side of his neck, he had a plastic bolt attached. He'd lost the one on the left somewhere, and I made a mental note to see if I might locate it. If I found it beneath either Hawthorne's or Viola's body, I thought that would take me a far way to finding the perpetrator. Of course, his face, neck, and the tops of his hands he painted in greenish-gray tones to resemble closely the movie monster, but like the bolt and the wig, the paint was wearing away, especially at his neck where I assume he'd been rubbing himself. I made another mental note to see if I could spot any speck of body paint on either of the bodies, or on the candlestick someone had clobbered Viola with.

I wasn't much for lies, but I told a second fib over the course of as many minutes. "Sure. You look great."

He grinned again. It disturbed me.

"What do you do for work?" I asked.

"What word?"

"Work," I repeated. I slowed my speech and over-enunciated the word to offset the brain fog he was hearing through.

"Right. Where I work. Realty." He extracted a business card from a pocket. I took it by the edges to not smudge the fingerprints he'd just given me and looked at it. Based on the card, he not only worked in real estate, but was the president of his own company. Carefully, I placed the card between the sheets of the notebook near the spine so it wouldn't slip out. I would have preferred to drop it into an evidence bag, but not only would that seem suspicious, I didn't have one on me.

"Do you do a lot of business with Hawthorne?" I asked.

He sat in silence. For a moment, I thought the drink had taken him to dreamland. Eventually, he glanced around to see who might overhear us, then leaned forward again. This time, he leaned so far forward, the back legs of the chair lifted from the ground. Once again, I pushed him backward so he wouldn't fall. I didn't want that to happen. At least, not until I'd left the general area.

He leaned forward again, not as far, then dropped his voice. "Want to learn a secret?"

I nodded. "Of course. I love secrets."

"We were about to close a deal that will transform this town completely," he whispered.

"How? To me, he looks like he already has the most impressive property in the county."

Of course, I didn't know that for sure. I'd only seen part of the outside of the compound, and the few rooms I had permission to enter.

"No. I'm not talking about this place. I'm talking about the gold mine along the highway. There are lots of opportunities to tear down many of the ramshackle buildings and put up shiny new ones. A new bank, new office complexes, new restaurants, parking lots, and the like. Revitalize this town completely." He grinned yet again as he sat back. I began to hate that disgusting expression on his face.

"Wouldn't the town have anything to say about one person owning so much property?"

Danny picked at a nail, then flicked the dirt to the floor. "Not a word. Especially since there's a new town hall and a public library in the plans, too. Get the picture?"

I got it in color and in 3-D. Loren was right. It was all about the money.

"What about Loren's little diner?" I asked.

Danny started to snicker, then full-out laughed. "That diner will become a paid municipal parking lot with trails down to the beach. It will add at least a million dollars of revenue to the town coffers every year."

Loren hadn't mentioned anything about anyone buying the diner from him. I wondered if he even knew, or if the town was going to play the eminent domain card.

I took a moment to jot down some notes. As I did, I asked my next question. "Can you tell me anything about what happened to Hawthorne or Viola tonight?"

I waited for the answer, as I read what I'd just written. I looked up and realized I wouldn't get a reply. Danny had leaned back in his chair, chin on his chest, softly snoring.

"Great," I said to him, expecting nothing back.

"He never could hold his liquor," Frankenstein's bride said.

I looked at the woman whose name I still couldn't remember. She wore a long, flowing white gown, which contained random rips and frayed edges. Along the neck was an intricate tulle pattern, but that too looked in disarray. Her hair was the most striking feature. She had it styled in a high, wild beehive, teased and sprayed with a gray streak in an homage to the movie classic. Like her husband, she, too, wore makeup. Unlike Danny's green pallor, the bride went with a pale, almost luminescent, with a greenish undertone. She wore dark, exaggerated eye makeup, including heavy eyeliner and mascara, which gave the impression of deep-set and haunting eyes.

"If he really took out three bottles of wine by himself, he gave it a good fight," I responded.

"I'm Cody Cassidy," I said as I held out my hand, hoping she would take the bait.

She fell for my ruse. "Amy Ewing."

I quickly wrote her name on the next page. Amy. I at least had the first letter correct when I'd guessed before.

"Did you actually get any information out of him, or did he try to pick you up?" Amy asked bluntly.

"What?" Her question surprised me and dropped me into a defensive posture. Not that this was the first time I've had to deal with a jealous spouse.

"What did he give you? I saw him pass you something."

"Just his business card," I said, regaining my footing.

"The one with his private number?" Amy said, barely giving me time to answer before launching into the next question.

"Beats me," I honestly said. "I only glanced at it before I tucked it away. Don't worry though, I have no intention of contacting him."

Amy locked eyes with mine for a moment, then gave me a curt nod. "You have to understand, he has this annoying habit of trying to pick up women, especially when he drinks."

It wasn't my business. I only wanted to finish questioning her so I could move on to the lawyer.

"How long have you been married?" I asked. It wasn't pertinent, but I asked anyway, to regain my role as the questioner.

"Six years," Amy said. She picked up the two standing wine bottles, and as she discovered each was empty, she set them back where they were. She spotted Danny's full glass near his hand, took that, and drank down the contents. "You really should open the bar back up. It's not like Hawthorne's going to need to drink anymore."

"Can you run through what you experienced tonight with Hawthorne?" I asked.

She glanced at her husband, saw he was still out, and spoke.

"I don't understand what help I can give you. I'm sure you've heard the same story a dozen times tonight already. You were playing. The thunderstorm started going crazy, the lights went out, and all of a sudden, Hawthorne was down. You know when we can get out of here? I'd really like to go home."

With some effort, I threw her a half-hearted smile. "I get you. I'd love to leave too, but we're stuck here for a while yet." "Do you work with Danny at his realty company?" I asked.

Amy exhaled, then leaned over and undid her high heels and kicked them off. She draped her right leg over her left and began to massage her foot.

"No. I'm the bank president," Amy answered without looking back at me. "I should have worn my Nike shoes instead of these stupid things. No one ever looks at a person's feet, anyway."

"Right," I agreed. "Dress shoes can be annoying and uncomfortable. I can't stand them myself."

Of course, I found them annoying to where I didn't even own a pair. I only owned sneakers, cowboy boots, and flip-flops.

One of the benefits I found of being a country singer was high-end designer shoes weren't an expectation.

"Did you know about the real estate deal that Danny and Hawthorne were putting together?" I asked.

Amy let her foot drop to the floor and shook her head. "He told you about that?"

I nodded.

"He's such an idiot. There's no way he should discuss that project with a stranger."

"So, you did. Is it as big as he laid it out?"

Amy shrugged her shoulders and clammed up. "I'm not at liberty to say."

I put my notebook aside. "Brantley said y'all would cooperate with me."

"Brantley is another idiot. He and Danny could have dressed as twins tonight. Look, I don't know anything about Hawthorne's murder other than it's tragic."

"What about what happened to Viola? She didn't hit herself on the back of the head."

"No clue. It wasn't me, though. And it couldn't have been Danny."

"You're vouching for him? You've been together the entire night?" I asked.

"No. But I've kept him in sight. You know who would be his perfect alibi if he were to admit to it? Her."

Amy pointed across the room, where I saw Dracula speaking to Dorothy.

"Amelia? Why her?"

"I have no clue. But he's been talking her up all night. Surely, you've seen it."

I had. I remembered the look of irritation on Amy's face at dinner.

"What are you talking about?" Danny asked. Neither one of us noticed he'd woken and was ready to get into the conversation.

"About that tail you're always chasing," Amy said to him, a sharp edge in her voice.

Danny sat back in his chair, closed his eyes, and exhaled. "I'm not chasing any tail. Again, for the billionth time, you're my favorite and only tail."

"Then what about her? You're always talking about her." Amy raised her voice and changed her pitch on the last half of the sentence that I recognized as a beginning of an argument. I did the best thing I could at the moment, which was to grab the notebook, leave the lovers to their quarrel, and seek out Dracula.

When she saw me approach, Amelia stopped speaking in mid-sentence and scurried away. Dracula, who had his back to me, seemed uncertain about what to do, and took a step to follow her when I tugged at his cape and stopped him.   He turned, spotted me, and his shoulders slumped.

"Ms. Cassidy," he said, not even trying to give me the traditional Bela Lugosi accent.

"Mr...."

"Garrison. Claude Garrison."

"Can we talk for a few moments?" I asked.

"That depends. I understand you think you're doing a favor to Viola by getting statements, especially since she's unable to do the work herself at the moment, but you've got no proper authority here. Any statement you've gotten here tonight, any mediocre lawyer could get thrown out during a trial."

"Can I ask what you do, Claude?"

"I'm Hawthorne Harris' attorney."

"Interesting. I assume you don't know what happened here tonight?"

He nodded.

"Can you tell me who will inherit the estate and the business, and everything else?"

"I can't say," he said. "Before you ask, I can't say because

I've never seen his will."

"Do you know if he has one?" I asked.

"I believe so, but until it's brought forth and read, I can't really say for sure."

"What kind of cases do you represent him on?"

"Mostly lawsuits and contracts."

"What sort of lawsuits?" I asked.

Claude moved to a chair nearby and sat. "Oh, the usual. Frivolous lawsuits that always came out of the woodwork. Everything from employee lawsuits from his business to trip and fall claims from his properties. He once had a gardener try to sue him because the gardener was allergic to the flowers Hawthorne wanted planted. Can you imagine that? Why would you even choose to be a gardener if you're allergic to gardens? That one got thrown out of court pretty fast. My services were probably overkill. A good paralegal or even someone who has watched more than an hour's worth of a courtroom drama could have handled it."

"Are there any pending from anyone here tonight?"

"Nope," Claude answered immediately.

"How can you be so certain?" I asked.

"If it was one thing Hawthorne was excellent at, it was holding grudges. He wouldn't have anyone near here who had a lawsuit against him."

I took a brief note, then I put down my pen. "What about the contract side? Can you share anything about those?"

"That I cannot do. Most of those pending contracts are not in the public domain yet, so they'll stay a secret."

"What about the one where Hawthorne was attempting to buy up half the town?"

"Where did you hear about that? That one is under the strongest lock and key we have."

"Danny Ewing is currently under a stronger influence, and according to my sources, he's a bit of a tattletale."

Claude smiled at me. "So, he drank too much, and him and Amy spilled the beans."

"You got it. According to them, Hawthorne was in a position to revamp the town, at the expense of a lot of the people who live here. Is that true? New bank? Library? Some businesses razed to the ground and turned into parking lots while he adds another billion to his portfolio?"

"No comment." Claude shifted in his seat, and I guessed right then every word was as true as the sky was blue.

"Well, someone else should expect to make a ton of money. What about the construction of all these new buildings? Who would do that?" I asked.

Claude mumbled something that I didn't quite hear, so I asked him to repeat what he said.

"Hawthorne Construction won the bid for any construction regarding the project you're talking about," Claude answered.

"Hawthorne Construction? I thought he was in the sardine business."

Claude chuckled. "Have you never heard of diversification? Hawthorne was into much more than sardine canning. He owns a fleet of boats to catch them. And a printing firm to print the labels, along with magazines, and anything else a client needs. Along with sardines, his plant also cans fruits and vegetables. He also owns a car dealership through another name, two restaurants, and a large construction firm that can handle everything from putting in roads to erecting an outhouse."

"He brokered a deal to buy all the land, then got the contract to rebuild the town? Sounds like he was double dipping in the deal."

Claude waved a hand at me. "Doesn't matter. It is all above board, and perfectly legal."

"Can you think of anyone in a competitor's construction company who might have not been so happy with the deal?"

Claude thought for a moment. "I'm sure there were several.

There are winners and losers in any bid. As I recall, there were a dozen firms who submitted bids, but Hawthorne's company beat them all."

"I'm sure they did," I said. "Is there anyone in this room who will either benefit greatly or get destroyed by any deal Hawthorne was involved in?"

Claude winked. "You're the singer and amateur detective. You figure it out."

CHAPTER THIRTEEN

After Claude left, I found myself alone in a room full of people. Rather than seek someone else to talk to, I immersed myself in my thoughts as I reviewed the notes I'd taken.

The lights blinked out again. Rather than return right away, they stayed out. Someone moaned, and someone else muttered the words 'not again'. I'd always found solace in the quiet moments, and normally didn't mind the darkness, but this was different. Bad things happened every time the lights went out here, and I instinctively pressed into my chair that I hoped would protect me from a potential attacker.

As I waited, my heart thudded in my chest as I strained my ears, trying to catch any hint of movement or sound. The silence was as pressing as the darkness. In my mind, I counted the seconds off as I sat uncomfortably waiting for the lights to return.

Off in the distance, I picked up a loud thud, as if something had fallen. With my luck, it was a chandelier toppling from the ceiling, creating yet another mystery I couldn't solve. I overheard whispers but couldn't make out any words. A flicker of panic surged within me. My mind raced through all the possibilities of the lights failing so consistently. I didn't think it was the storm causing it. I'd remembered someone saying something about a backup generator, and if that kicked on, I didn't expect the power would still be so shaky. There had to be something else, and I wanted the lights to return.

Then I remembered I had a light in the back pocket of my jeans. I leaned forward and found Laurel's phone. It took me only a few seconds to turn on the built-in flashlight, and with that on, I at least saw my feet. I considered heading over Bozeman's way, but then it dawned on me that if I could see using the little light, the perpetrator could also see me. That thought overwhelmed my mind, so I turned the light off and shoved the phone back in my pocket. At that moment, I realized I had seen no other lights during the outages. Phones were so prevalent I couldn't do a single show without seeing at least a dozen pointing in my direction, but tonight, except for the bar-back, no one else seemed to have one. I wondered why.

I considered my next move as I internally counted off the seconds of darkness. Funny how the seconds seemed to stretch when one couldn't see. Then, with a sudden click, the darkness shattered as the room was once again flooded with light. Since the light had been out for an extended time, I blinked against the brightness, squinting as my eyes adjusted to the sudden change. I glanced around the room and noticed that everyone else seemed to be no worse for the wear.

I wanted to figure out what the sound was, and to do that, I wanted to get a little help, so I approached Bozeman and Laurel, who were still sitting together.

"How is Viola?" I asked.

Laurel looked down at her patient. "She seems to be sleeping. Breathing is fine, and I've checked her pulse periodically, and that's remained steady. She'll need a scan to determine if she has a concussion, but that will have to wait until we can get her to a hospital."

"You've done a good job with her. Thank you," I said.

Laurel smiled, but didn't respond.

"Did either of you hear that noise when the lights were out just now?" I asked.

"Sounded to me like a chair fell over," Laurel said.

Bozeman disagreed. "I don't imagine it was a chair. It sounded smaller, with not as much heft to it."

I considered it for a moment, trying to replay the sound in my mind, and I tried to determine the direction from which it came. Finally, it hit me.

"Come with me," I instructed Bozeman. I headed toward the stage with Bozeman right on my heels, and before we'd even gotten there, I saw what had happened. My microphone stand was lying on its side. I stepped onto the riser and picked it up. Concerned that my favorite Shure microphone had taken some damage, I examined it carefully, looking for dents or other issues.

"Codi," Bozeman said.

"I guess it's okay," I answered. "I can hook it up to one of the small amps and give it a quick test."

"Codi," Bozeman repeated. This time, something in his tone told me I should forget about the microphone for a moment.

I turned to face him. "What?"

He didn't speak, he simply pointed at my old wooden stool on which I usually kept my water, and an extra guitar pick or two if I dropped mine during a show. When I wanted to get down-homey with the audience, I would sit on the stool and play an acoustic number.

I glanced at the stool. My water bottle was on the floor, leaning against the stool's leg. Next, I saw the guitar picks scattered across the floor.

"Codi. Please, look," Bozeman insisted.

Finally, my eyes focused on the top of the stool. And there, lying innocuously on the round seat, was a single sheet of paper, folded in half. My heart raced with a mixture of curiosity and apprehension as I leaned to take a closer look. The paper was part of the set list I'd printed for Laurel, and someone had folded it so the song list showed on the outside. I unfolded the note cautiously, and my eyes widened as I read the stark message scrawled across the paper in bold, menacing letters: BACK OFF.

The words sent a chill down my spine, and my skin prickled with unease. I showed the note to Bozeman and set it back on the stool. I turned around and faced the room, like I was ready to give a performance, but instead, I studied the room and tried to notice if anyone was watching with interest, or if I could pick up any tell of who might have left me the love letter.

Someone tried to intimidate me, but that was a mistake. Because of my size, people had been trying to intimidate me for my entire life, but it wasn't going to work. Over the years, I'd grown a spine and an unstoppable spirit, both of which I was more than ready to use. I refused to be intimidated, refused to let fear dictate my actions. The note was simple, for me to back off. That meant to me I needed to double down and figure this thing out before I was the next person receiving a candlestick at the back of my head.

I took a deep breath, and I felt my resolve harden. More than ever, I was determined to uncover the truth. And I knew just where to start.

I left Bozeman on the stage, and I headed right for Brantley. He locked eyes with me when I was still several strides away. He attempted to step backward, but since he was at the edge of a table, he had nowhere to escape to.

"What's up, Brantley?" I asked when I'd got close enough for the tips of my shoes to touch his green boots.

"What… what do you mean?"

"I'm really curious about a few things, and the first of which is why the lights keep going out."

"It's a power fluctuation. We get them all the time when storms roll through. All the time," Brantley answered.

"We all live and work around here, and have gone through severe storms before, and we've never had a problem with the power grid," Loren said.

During my brief bout of tunnel vision, as I wanted to question Brantley, I hadn't noticed the group that had gathered. Loren was standing just to the left of me, and Amelia, Helen, Amy, and Claude gathered in a small semi-circle around Brantley and me. Perhaps they were expecting a good old-fashioned schoolyard fight. The thought crossed my mind as well, and I had to admit, I was ready if it came to that.

"No. I don't mean the grid itself," Brantley said. "I think I explained before that when there's even a second of power disruption, the automatic systems pop into place. The generator turns on, and the house locks down."

"Why?" I asked.

"Why?" Brantley repeated. Apparently, he was having trouble understanding my questions all of a sudden. He made me question if I had to slow things down for him and enunciate better, or if I had to get closer to his face.

"Why," I repeated. "Why does the house go into a full fortress mode at the loss of an amp of power?"

Brantley tried to move back, but encountered the table again. Instead, he boosted himself up and sat, trying to look nonchalant in the process. "I shouldn't say. Mr. Harris wouldn't like it."

I threw a thumb over my shoulder toward the body. "Honestly, I don't think he's going to object at all."

Brantley sighed. "Okay, okay. Several years ago, there was an incident here. A small group of thieves waited until the early morning hours, then cut the power at the main line. After they broke in, they held Mr. Harris at gunpoint until he opened his safe. They got away with money, jewelry that had been in the family for generations, and a couple of paintings. A Rembrandt and a Van Gogh, if I'm not mistaken."

"So that prompted the power to cut over?" I asked.

Brantley nodded. "And more. He hired a security company to do an assessment of the property. On their recommendation, Mr. Harris added the guard out front, along with a roaming night patrol. And the generator, along with an electrified fence. Rumor has it there are multiple safe rooms in the house now, but I know of only one myself. I also heard he added a huge walk-in safe behind a wall somewhere, but I've seen no evidence of that."

"After the robbery he became a paranoid recluse?" Loren asked.

"A recluse, no. Paranoid? Certainly. I think he would have added a moat filled with crocodiles if it wouldn't have been a potential eyesore."

"What about the thieves? They get caught?" Amelia asked.

"Almost immediately. And only because of their bad luck. A local cop had pulled over a speeder, who had turned into the driveway to get off the road. The thieves, in their hurry to escape, plowed right into the unlucky speeder's car."

"I didn't know about that," Claude said.

"No one did. Hawthorne feared if people knew, he'd be even more of a target. So, he buried it deep. He even managed to keep it out of the papers," Brantley said.

"To get back to my original question, what's the deal with the lights?" I asked. "Even if the generator didn't get wired correctly, I wouldn't expect that the power would fail so much. And it's doubly suspicious that every time the lights go out, something bad happens."

"Unless there's someone standing over there by the switch." I looked at the doorway where I expected the light switches to be, just like every other building on the planet. There weren't any. It was the only entry into the room, so I didn't bother looking elsewhere other than where they should be. "Where are the light switches?"

"There aren't any in this room," Brantley said, like it was a logical answer.

I rolled my eyes. I was growing tired of having to ask questions to people like I was interrogating a group of five-year-olds who didn't speak English.

"Look, Brantley. Stop with the word play. If there aren't any light switches in this room, how are the lights controlled? I can't imagine they just stay on until all the bulbs burn out."

"There's an app for the lights in this room that Mr. Harris uses."

I stared at him, hoping he'd get the hint that he should expand on his answer, and eventually he did. "When Mr. Harris made the security improvements to the house, he also added technology to turn it into a smart house. Cameras, an app to control the lights and temperature, that sort of thing. Surely, you've seen those commercials where people turn on the lights before they even get home? Or have those doorbells they can answer remotely?"

I was well on my way to frustration. "I don't watch a lot of television. Who has access to the app?"

Brantley stewed on it for a while. "Mr. Harris, of course. I have it. The security chief, and I believe the head maid."

"That's it?" I asked.

He nodded.

"Is that annoying dinner gong controlled the same way? Through an app?"

"Yes. The same one. It's quite remarkable. It can dim the lights, play audio, all kinds of things."

"Fascinating. Can I see your phone, Brantley?"

"No. I don't have it with me," he said.

"I find that hard to believe."

"No, it's true. Mr. Harris didn't like people having phones at his dinner party."

"Paranoia again?"

"No. He simply thought that people should live in the

moment and enjoy each other's company without doing so behind a phone."

"Laurel had a phone on her. So did the bar-back. So did Viola."

"He wasn't as concerned about the band. We should have checked the bartender, and we wouldn't have allowed the phone in had we found it. Heather has worked with us before. She knows all the rules quite well. They're all spelled out right there in the contract."

"And Viola?" I asked.

"Why, she's the police chief," Brantley answered. "She wouldn't have parted with it even if we'd asked her to. A call could come in for her at any time, and there have been events here where she's been called away on police matters."

That tracked with me. My dad was the same way. He always said he was a cop twenty-four hours a day, eight days a week, three hundred and sixty-six days a year. Even when on vacation out of state, he carried his badge and gun, just in case. Fortunately for the family, he never got pressed into service when he was enjoying his well-needed time off.

"What about the patrol?" I asked.

Brantley didn't answer at first. Once again, he looked at me as if he hadn't heard the question.

"You said before at night there were roaming night patrols. Why hasn't anyone come to our rescue?" I pushed.

"The gate closed and locked. No one will get in until it's unlocked." Brantley said.

"What about the guard at the shack? That was inside the gate, wasn't it? I seem to remember driving through the pillars, then down the road for a spell before we got to the guard. He was well within the gate. What happened to him, Brantley?"

"I don't have an answer to that question. You're right. The guardhouse is always manned, and as soon as the compound went into lockdown, he should have been in here."

"Where is he, then?" Helen asked.

I glanced at Helen when she asked the question. She looked like she'd come down some since I'd last talked to her, but her eyes had reddened, and her complexion seemed a little off. I assumed she was in the middle of a crash.

"Good question, Helen," Amy added. "Where is the guard if there's someone always on duty? We've been stuck in here for literal hours now and no one has come to get us."

Brantley shook his head. "I'm sorry, I can't tell you. I've been here with you. All night. I don't have knowledge about anything going on outside of this room."

"And you've got no way to contact the guard?" Claude asked.

"We could try the land line again," Brantley said, pointing to the phone he'd try to use earlier.

"What's the number?" I asked.

"It's on speed dial. 8911."

I turned around and yelled to Bozeman across the room. "Boze, see if that phone works, will you? Try to get the guardhouse." I gave him the number and watched as he ambled to the phone and picked up the receiver. He put it to his ear and jiggled the hook switch a few times. He replaced the receiver and shook his head at me.

"I guess we're still cut off from the outside world."

"Unless we leave here," Amy said. "Why can't we just leave? Get in our cars and go?"

That was an excellent, simple solution to the problem.

"What about it?" I asked. "Could I send Bozeman out to get help?"

Brantley frowned, then shook his head. "I wouldn't advise it. He electrified the fences. The best we can do at this point is wait until daybreak and have someone stand by the gate and see if they can flag down a passing car."

It wasn't the news I wanted, but was the news I got, so for

now I had to live with it.

Some of the others had additional questions for Brantley, but I stepped away, my brain processing what I'd recently learned. As I headed back to the stage to talk to Bozeman, I surveyed the rest of the room. Laurel still sat next to Viola, diligently watching over her. Danny appeared to be sleeping off his wine, and based on the way he slumped in his chair, he would wake with the backache of a century. Jackie wasn't in the corner I'd left her in. She'd moved to another seat farther down the wall, between where she'd sequestered herself in the corner and the stage. Hawthorne still lay where he'd fallen, which, I thought, was a good thing. The last thing I needed to deal with was a zombie running amok.

I took another three steps forward, then stopped in my tracks. A question popped into my head. Why had Jackie switched seats?

CHAPTER FOURTEEN

Rather than heading right to Jackie and start up with my questions, I took a seat at a table nearby, and adjusted my chair so I could study her while I pretended to review my notes.

I started at the beginning of the notebook and turned the pages, stopped at each one for close to a minute before turning the next page. Although my head tilted down as if reading, I focused my eyes on Jackie.

To me, she looked like she fully recovered from the trauma of finding her fiancé dead on the floor. She no longer sobbed and appeared to be in complete control of herself. In fact, she looked downright bored, as if she were sitting in a bus station waiting for the eight-fifteen to Albuquerque. Her eyes no longer glistened with tears, and they occasionally darted around the room to take in everything else going on around her.

Jackie crossed her arms and uncrossed them again. She gave the impression that she couldn't decide how her body language would look to anyone else in the building. Like she tried a little bit too hard to play the role that she found herself in.

As to the other people in the room, she showed disinterest,

if not disregard for each of us, and showed no initiative to interact with anyone.

"What's going on? Are you checking her out?" Bozeman said as he pulled up a chair and joined me.

"Am I being too obvious about it?" I asked.

"No. Not really. I love the way you use the notebook as cover. Super discrete move," he teased.

I chuckled. I would always count on Bozeman to break the tension.

"What's the deal, Codi?" he asked.

"I finished talking to Brantley a moment ago."

"I noticed. So now what?"

"Something is bugging me about her. Can you see where she's sitting?" I asked.

"Of course. She's right over by the wall. I would point at her, but that might break your cover." Bozeman grinned at me. He enjoyed getting my goat occasionally.

"When I came back from interviewing the catering crew, I found her in the back corner. She looked like her world had ended, and I imagined for sure she would have an emotional breakdown. But now she's over in that chair as composed as can be."

"That's all? You're suspicious of her because she calmed down?"

"No," I said, a little louder than I intended. Jackie looked at us for a moment and suddenly took an interest in her fingernail. I dropped my tone. "I'm also a little suspicious because she switched seats. She spent most of the night in the corner, and now she's almost on the stage."

Bozeman rubbed his chin, finally getting my gist. "You think when the lights left, she planted that note and didn't make it back to her original seat before they returned?"

I nodded. "Something like that, sure. But plausible?"

"I'd say so. You going to ask her about her movements?"

"I certainly am," I said.

"Before you do, I'd go check out her first chair."

"Why?" I asked.

Bozeman smiled. "I assumed you were the one with the super observation skills."

Calming myself, I took a moment, and before I spoke. When I looked over to where Jackie had been. I didn't notice anything unusual at first glance.

"What am I looking for?" I asked, no longer desiring to figure the mystery out on my own.

"Does anything seem different to you about the table compared to the one next to it?" Bozeman asked.

I looked again. This time, instead of the chair alone, I expanded my view to the tables next to the chair. The table farthest away from the chair looked normal. I observed two candlesticks on either end, and its surface held two empty wineglasses. The black tablecloth draped over the table dropped halfway down to the floor. In contrast, the table next to the first contained a tablecloth that dropped to within an inch of the floor and looked askew from where I sat.

"I think I'm going to go for a stroll," I said.

Leaving Bozeman at the table, I headed for Jackie's chair. When I arrived, I sat down. I looked around the room to see if anything had noticed my trip, and when I saw no one looking at me, including Jackie, I took a peek under the table.

"Well, I'll be a daughter of a gun," I said to myself.

Obscured by the tablecloth was a picnic basket, with a stuffed terrier sticking out of the top. I reached in and extracted my find. I set the basket on the table, removed the dog, and looked inside. At the bottom of the basket was a cell phone, and I had a good idea of who owned it. I put the puppy under my arm, picked up the basket, and sought Amelia.

"Hey, I found something you lost," I said as I approached Amelia.

She looked at me, at the basket, then at the stuffed dog under my arm. "Toto! Where did you find him?"

"He was in the picnic basket, just like when I saw him earlier this evening," I said. "I also found something else."

I opened the basket and extracted the phone. "Is this yours?"

Amelia opened her palm, expecting me to hand the phone to her, but I didn't.

"You didn't confirm that this is yours. Is it?"

"Open up the front. My driver's license is in there."

I opened the front cover of the light purple case and checked. From a slot, I extracted the license and confirmed it was Amelia's.

"Can I have it back now?" she asked.

"Can we check one thing on it first?"

"What?" she said.

"If that app is on there to control the lights," I answered.

"I don't even know what the app is, so there's no way it's going to be on there," she said.

She offered a good point. I didn't know what the app was either, so I wouldn't recognize it if I were staring right at it.

"You mind if Brantley takes a look?" I asked.

Amelia shrugged indifferently. "I don't care. Knock yourself out."

I waved at Brantley from across the room, got his attention, and motioned for him to join us.

"What?" Brantley said in a huff when he got to us.

I handed him the phone. "Can you see if the app Hawthorne uses on the lights is on this phone?"

He took the phone from me and swiped a finger across it. "It's locked. How did you get this in here in the first place? You understand you can't have phones here."

Amelia shot him a coy smile, but didn't answer.

I grabbed the phone from him and handed it to Amelia. "Do

you mind?"

Amelia took the phone, entered her security code, then passed it back to Brantley. He accepted it, accessed the apps, and scrolled for a while.

"Yep, here it is," he said as he handed the phone back to me.

I didn't use a lot of apps, but this one wasn't one I recognized as being in the mainstream. "Are you sure? I've never heard of this before."

Brantley rolled his eyes at me. "Open it up and try it. Mr. Harris had it created specifically for this house. It's not on the open market."

I touched the icon that resembled a castle, and the app opened. Once it did, a little map opened up, and I spotted a blinking blue dot. I zoomed in on the dot and as I did; I saw the layout of the ballroom on the screen. Several icons appeared on the screen. I pushed on a light bulb icon, and when I did, a sliding scale appeared, with a bar all the way at the top. When I touched the bar and moved it down, the lights above dimmed. I pushed it back to full. I touched the icon next to it, and the gong sounded. Satisfied, I closed the app.

"This leads to my next question. Why is this on your phone?"

Amelia held out her hand, expecting the phone. "Beats me. Never seen it before. I didn't even realize it was on there. You caught what Brantley said. It wasn't something on the open market, so whoever put it on there needed knowledge of it. Knowledge that I don't have. Besides, if I was involved in all this, do you think I'd be stupid enough to leave the app on there, then put my phone where anyone might find it? "

She had a valid point. But, then again, she might be playing me for a fool.

"Okay. Then how did it get there?" I asked.

"I can't tell you. Like I said, I lost it earlier tonight."

"Do you mind if I hold on to it?" I asked it as a question, but

I didn't intend to give it back to her.

"Sure, but you have to do something for me. Try to call for help."

It wasn't an unreasonable request, so I activated the phone and attempted to dial 911. The call never connected.

"No luck," I said.

"Fine. Can you lock it again? I have information on there I'd prefer people not have access to."

I didn't think that was an unreasonable request, either, so I locked the screen, then shoved Amelia's phone into my pocket.

"Can I have Toto back now?" Amelia asked.

I hadn't realized I still had the toy under my arm in a death grip. Without comment, I handed her the dog and the basket.

"Thank you," Amelia said.

I wanted to keep my focus on Jackie, turned and took two steps before I stopped and turned back to Amelia.

"When did you lose your basket?" I asked.

Amelia thought about it for almost a full minute. "Actually, I can't quite put a finger on it."

"Did you have it at dinner?" I asked, already knowing the answer, since I'd seen it when I first met her.

"Yes. I'm one hundred percent sure of it."

"And then?"

Amelia considered it for another thirty seconds before answering. "I had it with me when we headed for drinks in the other room. I remember now. When we first came back here, just before your show, someone handed me a glass of champagne. I already had a glass, so I set the basket down next to me to take the glass."

"Why'd you set the basket down?"

"I had to put it down to take the other glass."

"Who gave it to you?" I asked, really wanting to learn the answer.

For the third time, Amelia thought it over. This time, the

pause was unbearably long. "It was a man. Might have been Brantley or Danny, but I'm pretty certain Claude gave it to me."

"How certain are you? Eighty percent? Ninety?"

"Fifty? Forty?" Amelia said.

Those weren't the percentages I wanted. "Okay, thank you."

At last, I left Amelia and strolled across the ballroom to where Jackie was sitting. She saw me coming, and I confirmed she was indeed playing me since, by the time I got to her, the tears started flowing again.

"Hey, you. How are you holding up?" I asked as I dragged a chair over and sat in front of her, knees to knees.

Jackie sniffed once, then again for effect. She didn't fool me, but I let her think she had.

"I'm doing the best that I can considering… everything."

"Why did you move to here?" I asked, getting right to the point.

"What?"

"When I last talked to you, you were sitting in the corner over by the window," I said. I pointed in the general direction where I'd seen her last.

"I moved."

"Yes, I saw that. Why?"

Jackie's eyes moved from mine and appeared to focus on my right shoulder instead. I don't know what she was thinking, but I guessed it wasn't the truth.

"The storm," she said finally. "Every time the thunder pealed, the window shook, and I got scared. I moved here instead."

It was a possible truth, but her answer didn't totally win me over. "Why didn't you go sit with someone? There's an entire group of people here who I'm sure would love to keep you company. And offer you support, of course."

"No. These are all Hawthorne's friends and associates. I wanted to invite a couple of girlfriends of mine. Emily, from the gym I attend. She's my best friend. We talk every day. But Hawthorne said I couldn't invite anyone because he had only a certain number of seats available at the table."

"That's too bad," I said. I meant it. I'd seen people in that position several times over the course of my career. You put me on stage in any small venue where a group of people assembled, and I would always tell who the third wheel is, or who got a pity invite to the party. At the moment, Jackie was my number one suspect, but yet I felt empathy for her.

"That's true. I wish Emily was here with me now. I could really use her hug. She gives great hugs. You ever have a friend who gives great hugs?"

I nodded. Gibson will always be my go-to person for hugs, followed closely by Dolly, with Merle bringing up the rear. Gibson never failed to purr the second I picked him up. I could always count on Dolly to wrap her cute humanoid hands around my index finger. Merle loved to nuzzle my neck and occasionally mistook my ear for a grub. Fortunately, he only ever gave me playful nibbles.

"But Hawthorne said no. Emily couldn't come to the party."

"Did that make you angry?" I asked, looking for a motive.

"At first. But then, when he said you would be here tonight, that made up for it. After all, I'll see Emily at the gym tomorrow, right?" Jackie explained.

Unless she landed in jail.

"Did you have any other problems with Hawthorne? Any fights about marriage, or money, or living arrangements, or anything at all?" I asked.

"We argue sometimes," she admitted. "Every couple does. Usually just about little things about what to have for dinner, or what dress he wanted me to wear to whatever event we went to. It's always easy for a man, you know. They just have to put on a tuxedo and shiny shoes. We women have to worry about the right dress, and shoes, and jewelry. And perfect hair, and fancy nails, and smelling good. All that stuff, you know?"

I didn't really know since I always had my performance persona to slip into and it never involved a dress. In my closet, pushed all the way to the side, stuffed in a garment bag, was my one dress. Knee length, and black of course, so I could wear it to one of the two events I had it for, either a wedding or a funeral. No fancy shoes, though. That's why I had short black boots.

"Do you think I did this?" Jackie whispered.

"I'll give it to you straight. You're certainly a suspect. And near the top of the list."

"You know, there's someone in here who had a big grudge against Hawthorne."

"Who?" I asked.

"Amelia Brown."

That name surprised me. "Really? Why her?"

Jackie leaned forward. "I was supposed to be Hawthorne's first wife, but I wasn't his first fiancé."

You're telling me he was engaged to Amelia before you two got together?"

"Yes."

Now I seemed speechless.

"Amelia never mentioned that to me." I admitted.

"I'm not surprised," Jackie said.

"Were they together long?"

Jackie smoothed the dress over her knees and removed a piece of black lint before she answered. "Three or four years."

"She was his fiancé? Not just a girlfriend?"

"Nope. She had an enormous ring on her finger from him."

"You're sure?" I asked.

Jackie smiled, then wriggled the ring finger of her left hand. She wore at least two carets on that finger. "I'm sure. It looked exactly like this one."

"No way," I said. "That's the same ring? He took it off her finger and put it on yours?"

"Yes. It was his mother's. Or maybe his grandmother's. I forget which."

"Do you know what happened between them that caused the breakup?"

Jackie shook her head. "Not entirely, but I have my suspicions."

I waited a beat for her to fill in more information, but she didn't get the hint.

"What were they? Your suspicions? Did they have something to do with her being his accountant?"

"No. Amelia is a strong, independent, capable woman. Hawthorne is one of those old-fashioned men. And by old-fashioned, I meant it in the Biblical sense. Women should stay seen and not heard. Should be happy in the kitchen and be a baby incubator. I think Amelia bit off more than she could chew when they got together. I've heard she tried her best to play that role, but in the end, she wouldn't do it. Amelia is too much of a modern woman to put up with his mindset for too long."

"She broke off the engagement? Not him?" I asked.

"That's what the rumor was around town. And since it's such a small town, that rumor spread around like a wildfire."

"How did he take that?"

"He tried to destroy her career for making him look bad. Threatened to take his business to other firms, and trust me, that would have sent her firm from riding high on the hog to right into the toilet."

"But yet she's still his accountant?" I asked. "And through all that, he still invited her to this party tonight?"

A small smile traversed Jackie's face. "That's where I came in. We met when he was still with her, and it didn't take long to get this ring onto my finger."

"He invited her here to make her jealous?" I asked.

Jackie nodded. "He had a mean streak that way."

"Why did he keep her on then?"

"Because I think he's still sleeping with her."

That comment caused me to do a double take. "What? Do you know that for sure?"

"They worked a lot of long nights together, and usually when they did, they met at his office. Anyone else, they came here. He needed something from Danny, Loren, or even Helen, and they came here. To his office upstairs. But Amelia? Her, Hawthorne left the house for. That doesn't quite add up, does it?"

It did not to me, and I wanted to go back and ask Amelia a few follow-up questions. I got up and made my way halfway across the room. Just as I hit the exact center of the room, the lights went out. Again. This time, I reacted and pulled Amelia's phone from my pocket, intending to use the app to turn the lights back on. I opened the phone, encountered the lock screen, then shoved the phone back in my pocket. Before I could pull Laurel's phone out and activate the flashlight, I heard a crash behind me, and a muffled squeak that sounded like a large mouse.

I moved back toward where I left Jackie, misjudged my steps, and ran right into a table, knocking the wind out of me.

It took me a couple of minutes to regain my composure, and when I was ready to resume my march, the lights suddenly lit and I could see again.

Jackie's chair sat empty.

CHAPTER FIFTEEN

I figured Jackie must have gone somewhere, so I turned in a complete circle while searching for her. Unless she had squirreled herself away under a table or magically turned into a chair, Jackie wasn't in the room.

"Where in the world?" I said to myself. I spun in a circle a second time, just to make sure I hadn't missed her.

"What's going on?" Bozeman asked. "Is there a reason you're spinning like a top?"

"Do you see Jackie anywhere?" I asked.

Bozeman took a moment and spun in a circle himself.

"Nope. Perhaps she's over by the stage."

I nodded. The stage had a half-wall built on either side. Each wall only measured three feet wide by four feet high, but that still left plenty of room for someone to hide over there if they wanted to. I did the due diligence and headed for the stage.

I explored the left wing first. There, I discovered a stack of three cheap, vinyl-backed chairs. The kind I'd seen in conference rooms dozens of times. The chair on top had a slit through the seat, exposing the thin yellow foam beneath the brown vinyl. I suspected the other two also had damage of some sort.

When I moved to the right wing, my interest peaked when I noticed a black tablecloth covering something. I reached out and grabbed a hunk of cloth. I pulled with all my might, intending it to float free, like that trick where someone removes a tablecloth from a full set table and doesn't disturb a thing. That's the way it worked in my head. In reality, it didn't come free.

I yanked again and got the same results. Clearly, it snagged on something. I took a less impressive approach, found an edge, and worked the tablecloth free. When I finally had it released, I discovered the treasures beneath. Three crates of items. The top crate held a box of light bulbs for the chandeliers in the ballroom. I didn't bother to check what the other two contained since they were too small to hold Jackie. I dropped the tablecloth without covering the crates and returned to Bozeman.

"Well?" he asked.

"No luck. Did you spot her?"

He shook his head. "Neither hide nor hair."

"Okay. I'm going to go check the other rooms."

"You want me to go with you?" Bozeman asked.

"No. I'd like you to stay here in case she reappears. And keep your eyes on Amelia, too, since I want to have a friendly chat with her when I get back."

"Which one is Amelia?" he asked.

"The one dressed as Dorothy."

Bozeman nodded without speaking, and I left the room. The first place I checked was the room Heather and her crew were hanging out in. I stuck my head in the door, not wanting to get engaged in any conversation. Someone had brought decks of cards because they had broken into two groups and were playing a card game I didn't recognize. It didn't take me long to notice Jackie wasn't among them.

I did a lap around the area I was familiar with. The gym was devoid of people. I checked the doors leading to the outside and found them locked. I thought that might be a fresh development, but I didn't remember if I'd checked them before to tell if they opened or not. They had at some point, since Bozeman ran out to the bus for fuses, and Heather accessed her truck. Since I didn't know if the door locks were automatic on shutdown, I made a mental note to ask Brantley.

I left the gym, and my next stop was the bathroom. Although I expected the room to be occupied, when I turned the knob, it freely rotated and I pushed the door open, turned on the light, and found it empty. I noticed the towel was crooked, so I reached out, touched it, and found it still damp from someone who had recently washed their hands. Another mental note, this one to ask Bozeman who he'd brought recently, passed into my brain. I righted the towel, shut off the light, and left the room.

The only thing left for me to do was take another trip down the hallway, and I did. I made my way up the left side, checking each knob as I walked. None of them turned. I got the same result with the door at the far end of the hallway and most of the doors on the way back. Until I reached the last one. To my surprise, that knob turned.

I took a deep breath, then pushed the door open. To my satisfaction, it didn't squeak like in old horror movies, and it opened all the way until the door encountered the stop. I brushed my hand along the wall next to me, hoping to encounter a standard switch, and when I hit it, I turned on the overhead lights. Where the chandelier lights were classic and comforting in the ballroom, what I turned on was anything but. Overhead, bright lights shone through plastic panels, giving the room an ambiance impression like that of a clinic or a warehouse.

I'd stumbled into a storeroom. The room was approximately thirty-feet square, and each wall held floor-to-ceiling wood shelving units. I couldn't identify the wood, but I recognized the scent as cedar. To my left were shelves packed with everything needed for a fancy dinner service, like the one I'd witnessed.

I stepped to the shelf and saw rows of water and wine glasses. In addition to the wineglasses, beer mugs, and rocks glasses sat among the shelves. Next to the massive display of glassware sat the china. I counted six unique patterns of dinner plates, salad plates and bowls, soup bowls, coffee saucers and cups, and those little plates people were supposed to use as bread-and-butter plates. I picked up a dinner plate and grunted at the heft. Personally, I preferred melamine since it was light and didn't break whenever we forgot to secure the cabinet and Bozeman made a sharp turn. Granted, it wasn't made for the microwave, but that's why we owned various containers made for that job. So, what if they were all spaghetti stained?

Past the china, I came to several large boxes. I opened one and found the silverware. Based on the box, I guessed it was the good stuff, and when I picked up a fork, the weight confirmed it. What was the rule? The heavier the fork, the tastier the food? Perhaps I made that up. I inspected several boxes. All held silverware, again in distinct patterns and alloys. One box held nothing but serving utensils such as fancy meat forks, actual metal ladles, and tongs in several sizes. Not a speck of plastic anywhere. Clearly, Hawthorne Harris would have detested a meal served on my bus.

The back wall, although covered with shelves, contained only cloth napkins. I counted six shelves from bottom to top, and each shelf contained napkins in a separate color. I picked one up at random, Burgundy red, twelve inches square, in a thickness that seemed wasted on a napkin. Nothing unusual about it, so I refolded it the best I could and returned it to its place.

The shelves on the third wall contained all things decor. Candlesticks of various sizes, vases, trinkets, and do-dads galore. Chinese lanterns stood lined up next to foot-high crystal Christmas trees and a variety of wooden soldier nutcrackers. I seemed surrounded by something for every holiday. Glass shamrocks, red crystal hearts, even a porcelain Easter bunny that looked like an antique to me.

The center of the room held two wooden tea carts, one twice as large as the other. It was large enough to contain an interior compartment, so I opened the double doors and discovered nothing except what a mouse had left behind. It seemed even the rich had to deal with vermin occasionally. Smiling, I shut the doors. I moved to the door, turned, and looked around a final time. I'd found some interesting things, but not Jackie. Another mental note for Brantley passed into my head, this one to see if he had keys to the remainder of the house so I could snoop around a bit more.

As I sighed, I turned off the lights and closed the door before me. I tried the knob again, and it turned easily. Someone had unlocked the door and left it that way. It added another question to my growing list.

My search for Jackie had failed in underwhelming fashion, so I returned to the ballroom to have a chat with Brantley about the keys and Amelia about her supposed affair.

I spotted Brantley first, standing at the bar and having an animated discussion with Ashley, whose arms-crossed posture told me she wasn't having anything he was ranting about.

"What's going on?" I asked.

"I'll tell you what. She's refusing to serve me a glass of wine," Brantley snorted. He didn't seem happy. I didn't feel sorry for him.

"You agreed to that. No more alcohol tonight. Remember?"

He scoffed. "It's only wine. That's barely alcohol. It's Californian, for grape's sake."

I wasn't sure how those things connected in his head, but at the moment, I wasn't interested.

"Do you have keys for this place? I can't find Jackie, and she's nowhere that I can actually access. I'd like to check the entire house for her."

Brantley shook his head. "No way. Mr. Harris wouldn't like

that at all. No unauthorized person in restricted areas. That's the rule."

"Is this a secret government facility? You talk like it is. Besides, Mr. Harris won't care because he's too busy waiting for the coroner to arrive. You promised that you'd cooperate with me, and frankly, it's a promise that several people have broken several times tonight. I'm getting tired of it. You going to give them to me, or not?"

Brantley looked at me, then at the prone body, then back at me.

"I'll tell you what. I'll make it easy for you."

With purpose, I stepped around to the back of the bar, and as Ashley stepped aside, I saw what I wanted. From the wine fridge beneath the bar, I extracted an opened bottle of what I assumed was a cheap California wine. I placed the bottle on the bar top and pointed at it.

"A barter. A trade. The house keys for the bottle. The whole thing, all to yourself. What do you say?"

He thought about it for a good, long minute. Apparently, it gave him some trouble because I noticed several beads of sweat appear on his forehead.

"Fine," Brantley said at last. He rooted around in his tunic for the keys and slammed them on the bar. In one motion, he grabbed the bottle, gave us a sneer, and stomped away like a pouting toddler carrying a cookie.

"You know, he'll be right back," Ashley said.

"Why?" I asked.

Ashley held up the tool in her right hand. "That bottle has a cork in it."

I couldn't help but smile, and I did so. I even managed to laugh. It was only a short one, but it felt good. A simple chuckle had knocked away some of the tension I'd let build up over the course of the last few hours.

I was about to respond when the lights dropped out.

"Amelia, what's the password to your phone?" I called out in the darkness. She replied without hesitation.

As I reached for her phone in my pocket, I took a step to my left, caught the edge of Ashley's mat, lost my balance and fell. At that moment, I heard the loud report of a firearm, followed by several screams. I had dropped Amelia's phone in the fall and flailed my arms around on the floor until I finally found it. I punched in the code, opened the lights app, and ended the darkness.

"Are you okay?" Ashley asked as she leaned over me.

"I think so. Can you help me up?"

With her assistance, I got to my feet and took a second to regain my balance.

"Holy cow," Ashley said. "Look at this."

I turned and looked at where she had pointed. It was a small, round hole in the plaster, directly in line with where I'd been standing a second before the lights failed. My neck and ears got warm, which meant only a single thing. I transformed from happy-go-lucky Codi to overwhelmed and angry Codi.

Play time was over.

There was a new sheriff in town, so I strode to the middle of the room, and in my most commanding voice, issued an order. "Everyone come here and line up. Now."

"Why should we?" Claude asked.

"Because someone took a shot at me, so do it."

Loren stepped forward first. "Come on, folks. Let's go."

Reluctantly, everyone lined up, including Stacy and Ashley, who stood in line but a step away from those in costume. Except Danny Ewing.

"Bozeman, can you go search him? See if he's really asleep or if he's pulling a con. Oh, and if he's armed."

Bozeman nodded and headed for Danny, who remained in the same position I'd seen him in for at least two hours. I watched as Bozeman did a quick search of Danny's person, and finding nothing, let Danny sleep and returned to the line.

"Here's what's going to happen. If you have pockets, empty them, then you'll get a pat down search."

"No way, I don't want him touching me," Amy said, pointing at Bozeman.

"Fine. Bozeman, you take the men. Laurel, please take the women. Start with Ashley and Stacy."

"Why them?" Helen protested.

I shrugged. In my mind, they were both innocent, so I knew I could exclude them immediately. I also knew it would irritate the rest of the group if the hired help got to go first for a change.

Laurel walked in front of the line and got to Ashley first. When she emptied her pockets, Ashley produced a bottle opener and two corks. Laurel did her TSA impression, patted her down, and said she was good. I nodded, and Ashley returned to the bar.

Stacy, next in line, had nothing in her pockets, and the pat down revealed nothing.

"Where's your phone?" I asked, noticing she didn't have it on her.

Stacy gestured to the wall where she'd been sitting most of the night. There, on the floor and plugged into an outlet, was her phone. I nodded, and she left the line.

"I'm next since I've got nothing to hide," Loren said as he stepped out of line and approached Bozeman. Loren removed from his pockets a wallet and a set of car keys, got patted down, then received the green light to sit down.

"This is ridiculous," Claude said.

"Think so? Then you can be next," Bozeman said.

Claude made a noise similar to a growl, but he stopped with the theatrics the second Bozeman got close to him. Like Loren, Claude carried keys and a wallet. He also carried a pocketknife, which Bozeman slipped into his own pocket, vowing to return it when the night's festivities were complete.

Brantley was the easiest of the men to search. He had a

single empty pocket and had nothing on him.

Laurel found Helen and Amy to be equally easy to search. Neither had pockets, nor anything on them. That only left Amelia, who, I finally noticed, was missing from the line.

"Okay, did anyone see where Amelia disappeared to?"

No one had an answer to the question.

"All right then, does anyone remember seeing her before this latest round of lights out?"

Claude tentatively raised his hand. "I did. I was talking to her right before."

"About what?"

Claude shrugged. "Not much, really. Small talk. Weather. Business. That kind of thing."

"Did anything seem unusual about the conversation? Was she distracted, or anything?"

"Unusual, like holding a handgun while we talked about the storm?" Claude chuckled. "No. She seemed fine. Maybe a little bored, but I can't blame her there. I am too. Given my druthers, I'd have been out of here right after the pie was served."

"What happened next?" I asked.

Claude rubbed his chin. "Well, both of us grew bored with the talk. I could tell. It was like a bad first date. Ever have one like that? Things go okay at first, but then you get that knot in your stomach and things go downhill from there? Become awkward? That's what it felt like to me. So, I left to find someone else to talk to."

"As simple as that?" I asked.

"Yep."

"You see anything when the power failed?"

Claude gave an extended exhale before he answered. "No. When things went dark, I was probably five or six feet away from her already. When it went dark, I stopped in my tracks, and didn't move until the lights came on."

He stopped speaking but looked at me for an extended few

seconds without dropping eye contact.

"Is there anything else?" I asked.

He moved closer to me. "I think I saw the gun fired."

Those were words I wasn't expecting.

"You saw the shooter? Who was it?"

"No, I don't know who the shooter was. It was way too dark. I think I saw the muzzle flash when it fired. Just a blip and it was gone."

"I don't understand."

"If I had my guess, I'd say something covered it, like a napkin, maybe?"

I thought about it for a second. I only carried a small firearm myself, and rarely fired it, but my dad would often take me to the range and practice with all sorts of weapons. Depending on the gun, it had a muzzle flash ranging from a sparkler to barely visible. Unless I dug the round from the wall, I couldn't tell what I was dealing with, but I liked where Claude headed with the napkin idea.

"Did you take the keys?"

I turned around. Ashley was there in front of me, asking the question.

"What keys?" I asked.

"The ones Brantley gave you. It didn't dawn on me until after I got back to my station after your lineup. Those keys were gone. Unless you took them, they're missing."

CHAPTER SIXTEEN

I sat down at a table and ran my fingers through my hair. Once again, I felt like I was missing something, or, in this case, several things, including two witnesses and a gun. I crossed my arms on the table and laid my head down on my arms, intending to rest my eyes for just a moment.

It wasn't long before I received a nudge. I lifted my head and noticed Laurel standing over me.

"Hey," I said.

"Have a nice nap?" Laurel asked.

"No nap. I only closed my eyes for a few seconds."

Laurel grinned at me. "How many seconds are in a half hour?"

"No? Really?" I took Laurel's phone from my pocket and checked the time. She was right. I dozed off. Clearly, I was more tired than I'd imagined.

"How's Viola doing?" I asked.

"There's some good news on that front. She regained consciousness for about ten minutes."

"Is she okay?"

"I think she'll be fine. Someone rang her bell pretty good. I asked her a few questions, and she knew her name, the current year, who the president is, stuff like that."

"Can I talk to her?"

"Sure. That's why I came over. She wants to see you."

I nodded, then stood. I guessed I'd really napped based on the way my back cracked the second I straightened my spine. After I stretched my arms over my head and flexed my legs, I was ready to go.

"Lead the way," I said.

I followed Laurel over to the table that Jackie had first used when I found her the first time. Viola was sitting up straight in a chair, a tablecloth draped over her shoulders like a blanket, and she held a plastic bag of ice to the back of her head. She smiled weakly at me when she saw me coming.

"Codi."

"Viola. How are you feeling?" I asked. I wanted to hug her, but she already looked uncomfortable, and I didn't want to add to it by squeezing her too hard.

"Like Humpty Dumpty. Like my head cracked open." She removed the pack and looked at the towel someone had wrapped the ice in. "At least, thanks to your friend, I'm not bleeding."

"Do you remember what happened in here tonight? About what happened to you?"

Viola returned the icepack to her head. "Just bits and pieces, and most of those are foggy. I remember several power outages, and that Hawthorne got killed. Did I ask you to get statements for me, or did I dream that?"

"It's real. You asked me to get statements from the service staff, which I did. When you… got assaulted, I expanded that and talked to everyone here."

Viola slowly nodded. "How did that work out for you?"

"Some people seemed helpful; others bordered on evasive."

Viola cracked a slight smile. "That sounds about right. Have any trouble or any primary suspects?"

"I had two people as my front runners, but they're both currently unaccounted for."

"You lost two people in a locked down house?" Viola asked.

I felt my cheeks redden. "Yes, I did."

"That's a first for me. What else do you have?"

I found a chair and spent the next several minutes recounting the events of the evening. Afterward, I retrieved my notebook and reviewed my notes with Viola.

When I finished, she nodded. "Not too shabby, actually. I'm surprised you got as far as you did. Clearly, you're your father's daughter. What's next?"

"My intention was to look for anything that may have gunpowder residue on it."

"Good plan. Perhaps I'll come along and help."

"No, Viola. You should stay right here," Laurel interjected.

Despite Laurel's advice, Viola dropped the icepack on the table and struggled to stand. To my surprise, she staggered three short paces before she almost fell. Laurel and I reached out almost as one and grabbed Viola's upper arms and guided her backward to the chair.

"I'm a bit dizzier than I expected," Viola admitted. "I'll wait here. You find anything. Bring it to me right away, okay?"

I nodded. "Will do, Chief. Laurel, would you mind staying here?"

"Of course," she said without a second of hesitation. "Go. Do what you need to do."

"You need any help? I've got a pretty good nose," Bozeman said.

"You know what I'd really love for you to do? Take a spin around the rooms you can actually enter and see if you can locate Amelia or Jackie. It shouldn't take you long, then you can come and join me."

"Consider it done. I'll be back in two shakes of a lamb chop,"

Bozeman said. He had his assigned mission, so he hurried from the room to accomplish it.

I scanned the area, deciding where to start. I returned to the bar and asked Ashley to move aside for a moment. Using my best guess, I stood with my back to the bullet hole in the wall and attempted to find out where the shooter stood. I figured they had done one of two things, either dropped the covering where they'd taken the shot, or carried it with them and disposed of it later. Mentally, I flipped a coin and chose to check the site straight ahead and work my way around the room counterclockwise.

The table directly across from me had a tablecloth, but it didn't look disturbed, and contained the requisite candlesticks and a wineglass. Nothing looked displaced, and I doubted in the time it took to take a shot at me, someone might have discretely removed the items, taken the shot, and reset the table. I realized at that moment, I only needed to check the settings that looked disrupted, much like how Bozeman pointed out the tablecloth that hid Amelia's basket. I followed the rabbit hole. If Amelia's basket held her phone, might it contain the missing gun as well?

Although the tablecloth looked undisturbed, I checked under the table. Nothing. I checked several tables, for both the scent of gunshot residue, and for Amelia's basket, but I found the same. Nothing.

When I arrived at the ballroom's corner opposite, I found two piles of napkins. The first pile was on the floor, hidden behind the table. I assumed people had discarded them after use. The second pile held a half dozen, still folded into neat rectangles. I took a seat behind the table, tried to be as discrete as possible in a room filled with people, and inspected the top napkin on the pile. It smelled like a tropical breeze, so I set it aside and worked my way through the pile. No luck.

I sighed, then looked at the floor, at the mess next to my seat. In my mind, I tried to justify the process of picking up each of those napkins and giving them the sniff test. Since they were dirty, I caught all kinds of scenarios in my mind. From the innocuous, someone picked up a napkin, wiped off the tips of their fingers and discarded it, to more uncomfortable scenarios. Spilled drinks, food remnants, sneezes. I didn't dive in with both feet, as I normally would with a task, instead, I moved the pile with my foot to make sure nothing hid beneath it, then, satisfied it held no secret treasure, I moved my chair and placed it over the pile. The police forensics lab could deal with it instead.

I sat for a moment, both to rest for a moment, and consider my next move, and it came to me in three quick bullet points. The missing keys. The gun. Amelia's basket. The thought of the gun reminded me to ask Viola if she carried a weapon, and if so, was hers still on her person somewhere. The shot at me and the assault of her would tie to a single perpetrator, if that was the case.

Break over, I resolved to do the easiest task and talk to Viola first, when I saw Loren and Claude talking to each other. It dawned on me that I'd seen them in various areas of the ballroom, and as I watched them, they looked like they were doing circles around the room's perimeter, like mall walkers getting their daily steps in. They rounded a corner and strolled in my direction. My intention was to wait until they passed before I got up so I wouldn't have to interrupt their walk, but they stopped just before they got to me when Loren grabbed Claude's forearm and stopped him.

"Seriously, man?" Loren said. His words came out as a low growl, like the way I'd expect a grizzly bear to sound if they would talk. "You mean we could still lose everything?"

Claude hesitated and looked to his left to see if anyone was within earshot. Since he didn't bother to turn around, he didn't see me sitting there as obvious as a bright yellow dot painted on a black canvas.

"Yes. It all depends on what the heirs to the estate decide to do," Claude answered.

"All of this nonsense tonight could be all for naught?"

"Look, Loren, you had a chance to go before the city planners to express your concerns, just like every other citizen in town at the open meeting we had."

Loren gave Claude a backhanded wave. "You mean the city planners who all have an individual stake in the plan? There wasn't a person on the committee who wouldn't benefit from these stupid plans. Revitalize the town! Ha! More like enrich the already rich."

"You're forgetting about all the additional tourists we'll get. People will stop here from all over. This won't be just a drive-through town on the way to anywhere else. Every business here will benefit," Claude said.

"Come on, man. Stop with the bull. I don't understand where you're getting all these additional tourists from. All the better surfing beaches are to the south, and all the great attractions are in either direction. You think people are going to flock here for the summer productions of Shakespeare plays they put on down at the Playhouse Theater?"

"Think of the new diner. You'll have lots of opportunities to make more money."

"How? By forcing me to move to the opposite end of town? I'm right on the main drag now, where I've made a name for myself for years. Do you think the tourists are going to want to inconvenience themselves by heading to the opposite side of town, which, by the way, won't receive a single fancy upgrade in buildings or services?"

"Concessions had to be made," Claude said.

"What about the people that work in my diner? Some of them live within a few blocks away and need to walk to work. They don't have the resources to buy a car to get to another location."

Claude shrugged indifferently. "Not my problem. That's yours. Perhaps you should pay them better."

From where I sat, I saw Loren clench and unclench his fists.

"I already have the best paying restaurant in town."

Claude shrugged again. "So, you'll have to hire new people. So what? It's the cost of doing business, and every business needs to deal with staffing issues. You're not alone here."

"This is going to ruin the diner," Loren said.

Claude laughed. "Hey, at least you still have the pies. You do most of your sales outside the diner. Pivot, Loren. Get a website. Go for expanded distribution. Find a way to reach out beyond your current delivery zone. You've got a great product, there's no reason you couldn't spread out to include of all of California. Or go regional. Or national, even. I'm sure there's a way. If they can get those New York cheesecakes all the way here, I'm sure you can discover a way to get a pie out there."

"I don't think you're understanding me, Claude. We're not talking pies. I'm talking about lives. There are people at the diner who depend on me for those jobs. And locals who have no other place to go for an inexpensive meal out."

"That won't be the case soon."

"Wait. What does that mean?"

Claude dropped his voice to just above a whisper, but I could still hear him. "When they build the new off ramps from the interstate, several new fast-food places are going in. People will have all kinds of choices. Burgers, pizza, fried chicken, sub sandwiches."

"I didn't know that," Loren said.

"Few people did. Hawthorne did, of course, and me, and the planners. Beyond that, no one. But again, it's a benefit to the community."

"Those new joints wouldn't happen to be fast-food franchises, would they?" Loren asked.

"Nothing unusual about that," Claude answered. "Most fast-food places are."

"Let me guess. Those franchises coming in are owned by

H.H. Holdings, Limited?" Loren said.

Claude didn't answer right away, and I couldn't see his facial expression since his back was toward me, but I could tell based on Loren's body language that he wasn't happy with whatever was on Claude's face.

"So, more truth finally comes out. That greedy pig cost me my prime location and was going to take away my employees and my customers." Loren growled.

Claude placed his hand on Loren's shoulder. "Look toward the future, Loren. What's past is past, and there's nothing we can do about it. Trust me, focus on your pies and you'll be fine."

Loren brushed Claude's hand away and leaned in toward him. "I've had enough of you, Claude, just like I had enough of your boss. Watch your step or you may end up just like him."

Without another word, Loren walked away toward the bar. Claude shrugged like he received threats like that every day, noticed Helen beckoning for him, and headed in her direction.

Alone again, I quickly rose and rushed back to Viola and Laurel. Bozeman was also there.

"I thought you were coming to help," I said to him.

"Well, I saw you over there not doing anything, so I figured you were done and didn't need me after all."

"I just overheard an interesting conversation between Loren and Claude," I said.

"About what?" Laurel asked.

"I'll tell you, but before I do, Viola, do you carry a sidearm?"

"Of course," she said.

"Do you have it on you?" I asked.

For a response, I expected her to whip it out of her side holster, but instead, she shook her head at me.

"It's locked in the glove compartment of my car. I didn't expect a shootout at a costume party."

She made a valid point; I thought. My dad often did the same thing when he entered places where he didn't expect to need a gun, which was usually smaller private events like backyard barbecues or Christmas parties.

"Could anyone have gotten it from there?" I asked.

Viola rooted around in her pockets and found her car keys. "Not without these."

That told me it most likely wasn't Viola's gun, which made things easier. Find the gun, find the owner, find the solution.

"Codi, what about Loren?" Bozeman asked.

"Apparently he may lose that diner of his," I said. "The way Hawthorne structured the land deal, Loren has to move to the other side of town, away from all the new developments."

"Why would he shut down because of that?" Bozeman asked.

"There are a bunch of new fast-food places moving in when they build the new interchange. You'll never guess who those new restaurants will be owned by."

"Hawthorne?" Laurel answered.

"Excellent guess. His entire plan included pushing Loren's diner to the other side of the tracks, quite literally. Viola, did you know about any of this?"

Viola shook her head. "I knew Loren was searching for other locations for his business, but he never told me why."

"Do you think he could have been the shooter?" I asked.

"Loren? No. I doubt it. It's not in his nature," Viola answered. "I've never even seen him with a gun."

"I have," Bozeman said. "Did you know he was a sharpshooter in the Army?"

"No. I knew he served, but he never went into much detail about it whenever I asked him. I got the impression it wasn't a good time for him," Viola said.

"It wasn't. But he loved to shoot. Earned several ribbons for it. When he got out, he did competitive shooting. I went to one once. Me, I consider myself no slouch around a rifle, but he impressed me that day. I don't think he missed a single bullseye during the entire competition."

"We should go talk to him," I said.

Bozeman frowned. "I assume by we you mean the two of us? You want me to go over and ask an old friend if he shot someone in cold blood?"

"Sure. What's the worst that can happen?" I asked. I smiled, but I guessed my charm wouldn't help. "He wouldn't shoot us, too, would he?" I was kidding, but it was a horrible joke that I regretted the second it passed my lips.

Bozeman looked hesitant based on his body language, but in the end, he relented. "Okay, let's go get this over with."

CHAPTER SEVENTEEN

We wandered over to Loren, Bozeman lingering a step behind. Normally he'd be right on my tail, but in this case, his stride matched his enthusiasm.

Loren, just finishing getting a glass of Coke from the bar, noticed us coming and headed for the nearest table. He sat and waited for us to join him.

"Bozeman. Codi. How's it going?" Loren asked. He drank from the glass and set it aside.

"Good, Loren," Bozeman said.

We both shifted into chairs and got comfortable.

"You have additional questions for me?" Loren asked.

"Tell us about your restaurant, Loren," Bozeman said, taking the lead.

He stared at Bozeman for an eon before, finally; he answered. "You know the full story?"

Bozeman felt his nod was enough of a clarification, but I wanted to make an addition. "We'd like to learn about it directly from you."

Loren took another drink, put down the glass, and turned it

between his fingers. The glass created a wet ring on the tablecloth, so Loren picked up the glass and set it in the ring.

"I overheard you speaking to Claude," I said. "Care to share the truth with us?"

Loren fell silent once more. After another drink, he began speaking. "It was all true. What you heard. The town is using eminent domain to take the diner from me. The plan is to build something new and shiny on my lot, like a parking garage or some such nonsense."

"They're going to pay you fair value for your property, aren't they?" I asked.

Loren shot me an expression that implied I was an idiot. "The bank was in charge of determining the value, so they took great liberty of determining what 'fair' actually meant."

"You're losing the diner for real?" Bozeman said.

Loren nodded. "Yes. In ninety days, I have to be cleared out. I found another location, but it's on the south side of town. Far away from the highway that remains the lifeblood for this city. It's also in an abandoned industrial area, so as you can imagine, there's not a lot of call for morning pancakes there."

"Will your clientele follow you?" I asked.

Loren's caramel-colored eyes met mine. "Not likely. Some will, but the retirees that don't drive? They'll find a more convenient place to eat."

"And it's unlikely that the tourists will go to your diner since it's far from anything else?" I asked.

"That's a fair assessment."

"Codi, let's skip right to the brass tacks, shall we?" Bozeman said. "Loren, did you shoot Hawthorne Harris and later take a shot at Codi?"

"No." Loren denied.

"No? Sounds to me like you had a good reason to hate Harris. And I know you tend to hold a grudge."

Loren jumped to his feet. The chair he sat on fell back and

crashed to the floor. He pointed a finger directly into Bozeman's face. "I didn't do it!" he yelled.

Bozeman, not one to be intimidated, took his feet as well, and headed into a stare down with Loren. I looked around the room and saw every face staring in our direction, so I realized I needed to deescalate things before the big boys got physical.

I stepped between the two men and held out a hand to each of them. "Come on, fellas, we had a nice civil conversation going. Why don't we head back to that?"

Bozeman glanced at me, and I gave him a light nod. In response, he took his seat. I leaned over and righted Loren's chair and invited him to sit. He did, took a drink, and regained his composure.

"I didn't do it. I couldn't have shot anyone," Loren said, dropping his voice to a notch under a normal level.

"Why not?" I asked, cutting off Bozeman, who appeared poised to ask a question.

"Because. Look at this." Loren held both hands out and attempted to make fists with each. I noticed as he did so, the pointer and ring fingers on each hand didn't fold into the balls with the other three fingers.

"What are you showing us?" I asked.

"I've got severe arthritis problems in four fingers. Halfway is as far as I can close any of them. I couldn't pull a trigger if I wanted to."

I stared at his hands as he continued to hold them out.

"You think I'm faking?" he asked. "Try to push them closed. I won't resist. Go on."

I moved closed and took the index finger of his right hand and tried to push it in toward the palm. "I'm not hurting you, am I?"

Loren shook his head. "Not really. I feel tightness, nothing more. Those joints are swollen, so you won't get any farther than that."

I applied more pressure and attempted to close the other three fingers with no better results.

Giving up, I turned to Bozeman. "I can't do it. You want to give it a try?"

Bozeman shook his head. "Not necessary. Loren, I'm sorry I accused you of this. I should have known you didn't do it." Bozeman held out his hand for Loren to shake, but Loren didn't extend his in return. Instead, Loren stood, moved around the table, and took Bozeman into a bear hug.

While the brothers reconciled, I returned to Laurel and Viola.

"That didn't seem like it went too well," Viola said.

I shrugged. "Ended up fine, and we can scratch another suspect off the list. I don't think Loren did it."

"Who did?" Laurel asked.

"Honestly? My money is on either Jackie or Amelia, and now that they've both disappeared, possibly both."

"Why them?" Viola asked.

"Jackie dropped on my radar first since she disappeared when Hawthorne got shot, and she stayed missing for an extended period. She didn't show up again until much later, and she switched seats when the power dropped and someone left me this love letter." I opened the notebook and paged toward the back, where I'd stuck the note between pages. "She also headed into some interesting emotional dispositions. When I spent time with her, or talked to her, she seemed to play the part of the grieving girlfriend, complete with plenty of tears and heartfelt sobbing. But when I wasn't with her, she took on the demeanor of someone waiting for a plane to board."

Viola listened, thought for a moment, and spoke. "That all seems thin. And circumstantial."

I didn't disagree, but since I wasn't a trained detective, I would only go with my gut.

"What about Amelia?" Viola asked.

"If you thought my case against Jackie was thin, you're going to love what I have on Amelia. I figured out that a phone app controlled the dinner gong and the lights. That app showed up on Amelia's phone."

"And she claimed she didn't know about it?" Viola asked.

"Of course. In fact, she claimed her phone was missing for most of the night. I found it under this table right here. Where Jackie hung out for most of the night."

"Anything else about her?"

"Jackie said she was involved with Hawthorne."

"You mean like in a personal relationship?" Laurel asked.

"That's what she told me."

"If that were truly the case, why kill Hawthorne? Why wouldn't Jackie or Amelia go after each other?" Viola asked. "Typically, in situations where a man is stepping out on a woman, the women will generally go after each other and leave the man out of the fight."

I'd read that somewhere. "That factoid never made sense to me. Why not band together and go after the man instead of each other? He was usually the instigator of the whole thing."

"Perhaps that's what happened here," Laurel said. "Maybe they decided to join forces and rub out the bad guy."

I considered it for a moment, and it certainly fell within the realm of possibilities.

"Is there anyone else you're thinking about?" Viola asked.

"No, not really," I said.

"Why not? You need to have reasons to exclude someone as a suspect just as much as you need reasons to include someone."

I smiled at the memory. "You got that from my dad, didn't you?"

"Yes. One of the first things I learned from him when we became partners."

"Okay. Let's run through them. I don't think Brantley is involved. No motive, and it's hard to be a personal assistant to someone six feet underground. I believe Amy and Claude are somewhat in the same boat as Brantley. They have too much to gain with Hawthorne being around, and now that he's not, I imagine they could both potentially take a financial hit."

I scrunched my nose, trying to remember who I left out. "Oh, I almost forgot about Helen. Personally, I think you ought to put Helen on your list as a probable drug dealer. I've heard from a couple of people tonight that she's been pushing things other than her personal training program."

Viola leaned toward and whispered. "She's already on my list. A person she's been selling to works for me. I'm hoping she'll lead us to her supplier, or anyone else higher up the ladder. Let's keep that between us though, I don't want her skipping town until I've had a chance to host her down at the jail."

Laurel and I both agreed to keep the secret.

"Okay," Viola said. "That only leaves Danny and the caterer's staff."

"I'd say you can ninety-nine and a half percent discount anyone involved with the caterer. Heather seems to have an excellent rein on her people, and I couldn't find one all night that had anything that resembled a motive. Danny, well, he's been on such a bender tonight. I'm sure he didn't do anything. I'm also sure he won't remember tomorrow he was here."

"That doesn't surprise me. He has visited me down at the jail. He has a tendency to close the bars and stumble around on the street until one of my officers picks him up. Danny needs serious therapy and needs to get himself into a program before it's too late, but I'd agree that he's probably in the clear."

The three of us floated in silence for a few minutes. Laurel broke it. "Now what?"

I ruminated on the question. "I'd love to find the gun. Especially since I know now that it's not Viola's. I'd also like to track down Brantley's missing keys, and of course I'd love to find out where Amelia and Jackie disappeared to."

"I couldn't find them," Bozeman said.

Surprised to hear his voice, I turned in my chair, and there he stood behind me off to my right side. "Just now?"

"Yep. You sent me on that quest, remember?"

"Did you check everywhere?" I asked.

"Everywhere I could, which wasn't much."

I nodded. "Then I guess finding the keys should be our top priority."

"Where did you find them last time?" Laurel asked.

"Brantley had them. I set them on the bar, then all of a sudden, I found myself under fire. I didn't even realize I'd lost them until Ashley said something."

"Maybe he took them back," Bozeman said.

That seemed logical to me, so I wanted to find out.

"Can I have your keys?" I asked when I got to within three feet of Brantley and his almost empty bottle of wine.

"You already have them," he slurred. He picked up a bottle and waved it in my face. "Even trade, remember?"

"You didn't take them back after I got shot at?"

"Nope. Except for your round up, I've been here the entire time. Although, I'll help you look for them, provided you secure me another bottle of wine."

I decided against it and returned to my group.

"He doesn't have them," I said.

"Let's go search then. Should we check people too, or just places?" Laurel asked.

"Start with things. Don't bother them until you've exhausted everything else. It could be they just fell on the floor by the bar, or someone noticed them and set them down somewhere," Viola said.

"All right, so that's our plan, then. Laurel, you go left. Bozeman, you go right. I'll head back to the bar. Viola, you stay here and check under the table next to you. Everyone got it? Good. Go."

We disbursed, and I headed to the bar. Viola seemed right to me, and the most logical thing was they fell to the floor where I'd last seen them.

"Hey Ashley, how's it going?"

"I wish I were home."

"Me too. Did you see those keys?"

Ashley shook her head. "Nope. I checked everywhere back here, too, just in case I picked them up on accident to clear the bar."

"Did you check underneath?"

"No. Let's do it."

Ashley released the brakes of the bar and gave it a light push forward. It moved with ease, and when it was a few feet away from its original position, she stopped.

I glanced at the floor and spotted a black straw, a wine cork and the screw top from a bottle of some sort.

"So that's where that went," Ashley said as she scooped up the top. Then she grabbed the straw and the cork and dumped them all into a trash can. "Satisfied?"

I nodded. It was a long shot, and it didn't pan out. I sighed, then helped Ashley push the bar back into place, even though Ashley could handle it herself. Once back in place, I moved on, checking random tables as I passed them to make sure they weren't hiding any secrets.

Eventually, I made my way to the stage area. I did a quick visual inspection. Everything looked the same except Bozeman's acoustic guitar looked slanted in its stand. I did a quick check of the wings, discovered nothing, and intended to rejoin Laurel and Bozeman.

I stopped. Bozeman never left his guitar slanted. Well, he did once when we played at a county fair gig several years before. He'd reached for it in the dark before a new song, and because he hadn't seated it correctly in the stand, he pushed it over onto the floor instead of grabbing it. When the lights returned, it took us a minute to get back on track while he performed a quick inspection to ensure everything worked fine. Since that day, he lined that guitar up in the stand as if it were a compass needle pointing north.

I picked up Bozeman's guitar and noticed right away something was off about it. I turned it flat and picked up a simultaneous jingle and thump inside. Then I shook it for good measure, and that action confirmed my suspicions when I saw the tip of a key over the sound hole. Not wanting to damage the guitar, I turned the tuning pegs to loosen the strings, then fished the keys from the hiding spot. I returned the guitar to the stand and myself to the group.

"I found them," I announced after Laurel and Bozeman rejoined Viola and me.

"Where?" Laurel asked.

"Over by the stage. By the way. Bozeman, you're going to need to check the tuning on your Martin."

He gave me a confused look, which I expected.

"You can do that if we ever get back on the bus. In the meantime, let's you and I go for a walk."

CHAPTER EIGHTEEN

Armed with the keys, I had a renewed sense of purpose and a hope that I'd finally get some of the answers I'd been searching for.

With Bozeman on my tail, I headed to the corridor near the bathroom, stopping long enough to check if Amelia or Jackie were involved in the poker game. They weren't.

"Why don't we look in here, first," Bozeman said when we neared the bathroom. He opened the door, slipped in, and I heard a click behind him. He wasn't keeping secrets, and I knew exactly what he was doing in there.

While I waited for him to relieve himself, I opened the door to the storeroom opposite. Upon first glance, nothing had changed. All the plates, glasses, and silverware sat right where I'd left them. The napkins looked all neatly aligned, except for the one I'd messed with and didn't fold exactly the way the others were. The decor stood all in place, waiting for holidays that would no longer come for Hawthorne. For a brief moment, I wondered if all these tacky treasures would remain with the house and the new owner, or if they'd end up in the discount bin at the local thrift shop.

That thought triggered another, and I pondered if Hawthorne himself had ever been in this room. I'd read somewhere a bunch of anecdotes of people who worked for rich folks and how the wealthy couldn't do the simplest of things, like operate a vacuum cleaner or make an omelet. Of course, the way it got spun in the article was those lucky, wealthy people did nothing that didn't add value to the bottom line, which, to me, made little sense. I hoped I never got so wealthy that I didn't want to butter my own toast.

I left the room and found Bozeman waiting in the hallway for me.

He grinned. "Sorry. Business called."

"That's fine, Boze. You didn't see anyone else in there with you?"

"Nope, sure didn't."

"Your hands are wet," I noticed.

He lifted them and looked in time to see a drop of water fall from the right one. "Yeah. I washed my hands, as usual, and as I was about to grab that towel in there, I noticed it seemed a bit gross, so I didn't take it."

"Such a rough and tumble cowboy you are," I teased. "Wait here."

I returned to the storeroom, grabbed the napkin I'd already mis-folded, and handed it to Bozeman. He wiped his hands, gave the napkin to me, and without thinking, I took it. A natural response to accept something that someone hands you. But now, I had the hot potato, and I didn't know what to do with it. I considered returning it to the pile in the storeroom, but instead took the more adult route of putting it in the bathroom on the rack next to the single hand towel. I'd let whoever attended to the bathroom figure it out.

"You ready?" I asked Bozeman as I stepped back into the hall.

"Just waiting for you."

Keys in hand, I found one to unlock the door next to the bathroom.

Bozeman turned the brass knob and swung the door open. Darkness seeped out, so he flipped the switch and lit up the room.

"What in the actual world?" Bozeman said as he stepped into the room and off to the left so I could enter behind him.

As I entered, I inhaled and held it, stunned by the sight. Instead of regular lights, flickering electric torches ensconced in ornate holders illuminated the room. The torches cast shadows across walls adorned with suits of armor. The suits stood four along each wall, a total of sixteen in all, each on a two-foot-high platform made of stone.

"Rich people and their toys, huh?" I said as I stepped into the room's depths.

Since I was neither an expert nor student of medieval Europe, I couldn't identify which countries the suits represented, or when in history someone wore them. But to my amateur eyes, they looked authentic. Some gleamed, the polished steel reflecting the dim lights. Others carried the weathered patina of age. I could only dream about the owners and the bygone battles and valorous deeds the wearers had lived through.

"It seems a little ostentatious to me, to be honest," Bozeman answered. "Why would anyone spend their money on all this… stuff?"

"I don't know. Any chance anyone could be in these?" I asked. "Like Amelia or Jackie?"

"I doubt it, but you want us to check, so let's do it. You take that half of the room," Bozeman said.

I looked at the row closest to me, and there before me stood a mixture of suits. Among them were towering full suits adorned with embellished helmets and imposing breastplates to smaller, agile pieces from plate mail to chain mail. The first two suits I encountered progressed quickly as the pieces didn't contain a helmet, and the way they sat on the mounts allowed me to see no bodies were hidden inside. The third was a full suit. I stepped onto the riser, and lifted the helmet, revealing nothing but empty space. The fourth stood empty as well.

In the corner was a large oak barrel, and within the barrel stood a variety of medieval weapons, from lances to spears, to a single quarterstaff. Leaning against the barrel was a mace, complete with an aged leather strap. On the wall above the barrel, three swords hung. One looked like the type I expected Loren to carry as King Arthur, but I didn't recognize the others.

I checked the remaining suits, found nothing of consequence, and joined Bozeman back at the door where he leaned against the jamb, waiting for me.

"Should we get one? I'd could be a statement piece during our shows," he said.

"Put a cowboy hat and jeans on a tall shiny object that won't budge for an entire set? Nah, the crowd would get it confused with you."

Bozeman stuck out his lower lip and pretended I'd broken his heart by the comment, and playfully punched my shoulder as I left the room.

"Come on. Let's see what else we can find," I said as I approached the next door. I found the correct key on the third try. The lock clicked open, and once again, Bozeman took the lead, stepped over the threshold, and turned on the light.

"Holy cow," Bozeman said.

"Now what?" I asked, following close on his tail.

"There's no way you have a key for that," he said.

I didn't bother checking. We'd only walked three feet into the room when we encountered another door. This door was one I'd always associated with either banks or movies that featured break-ins of a government installation.

The vault door stood a few inches over Bozeman's head, and

a good four feet wide. Instead of an old-fashioned combination lock, a digital alphanumeric keyboard displayed on a screen inset to the door. I pressed buttons at random, counting as I went.

"A potential forty-character password? How long would it take to break that?" I asked.

"That would still be easier than these," Bozeman answered, pointing out two additional boxes on the wall beside the door.

"What are those?"

Bozeman sighed. "For fingerprints and a retinal scan."

"Holy cow seemed right on the mark. He must have something amazing in here."

"Probably the usual. Priceless artwork, hundreds of gold bars, and millions of dollars' worth of bearer bonds."

"Bearer bonds? What are those?" I asked.

Bozeman shrugged. "Don't rightly know. Saw it in a movie once. Are we moving on?"

"Might as well. Not getting in here unless Hawthorne has the password in his pocket, and he wouldn't mind us removing body parts to gain entry."

The door at the end of the hall was the one I was looking forward to the most. In my mind, it would open up to something fantastic, and whatever we found inside would magically bring all the pieces together and solve the night's mysteries. For good measure, I pictured a console with a big green button labeled 'END LOCKDOWN' so we could leave this irritating place for good.

I put the first key on the ring into the lock, turned it, and tried again. It didn't unlock. I tried the second key with the same result. Wanting to move it along, I glanced at the ring and jiggled them in my hand. I attempted to unlock the door with one key after another until I tried all twelve keys, then I cycled through them all a second time to make sure I hadn't missed one.

"I don't have the right key," I said.

"Yeah, I noticed. Maybe Brantley doesn't have access to this part of the house." Bozeman said.

"I guess not. Think we can get through, like if you do some Bozeman magic?"

I stepped aside to give him room, and Bozeman stepped forward. He rapped on the door a couple of times.

"Step back a little," he said.

He watched as I complied, then encircled the doorknob with his right paw, and slammed his shoulder into the door. During the impact, he made a noise I didn't recognize as a good one, and before I could suggest he stop, he shouldered the door again. After achieving the same result, Bozeman stepped back.

"Sorry. I'm not getting through there without an ax."

"Is there another way? Could we pick the lock, or take the door off the hinges, or slide a credit card into the thing like in the movies?"

Bozeman pointed to the door side opposite the knob. "Hinges are on the other side. We don't have access to your lock picks, and if you have a credit card on you, I'd be happy to try, but I can guess where it is."

I gave him a half-smile. "Would your guess be that my credit card is in my wallet on top of the desk two feet above the drawer where I keep my lock picks?" I asked.

"It would," he answered.

"Then your guess would be a winner. I guess we will move on. We can ask Brantley about this door when we return to the ballroom."

Together we walked to the next door, and this time the lock yielded to the power of the seventh key I tried.

Bozeman, ever chivalrous, stepped into the dark void first.

"There's no light switch," he said. "It's dark in here."

"Don't worry, I'll save you." I retrieved Laurel's phone from my pocket, found the flashlight function, and after illuminating the small space for thirty seconds, I realized where we were. "Stay here. I'll be right back."

Using the light, I spotted a bit of reflective tape and followed it up three steps. I located a console, and after a few seconds, found the controls for the lights. After getting acquainted with the machine, I slid the controls up, and as I did, the canned lights in the room lit up. I stepped from the booth and rejoined Bozeman.

"Of course, he has his own theater," Bozeman said as he stepped farther into the room.

Before us was a three-level theater. For seats, we had a choice of a single seat, or a two-person love seat. Bozeman sat down in the chair closest to him.

"This is nice. Full leather." He fiddled with the buttons on the side, and I watched his feet go up and his back recline. "Oh, these have heating and cooling as well. And to think we've been sitting in those uncomfortable ballroom chairs all night. How did you know this was a theater?"

"I worked in one briefly while in high school. Of course, it wasn't as nice as this one."

"I can just imagine you in a little tuxedo with a red bow tie," Bozeman said. "Put on a film. Got any popcorn?"

I shook my head at him and looked around the rest of the room. "I'm going to check if anyone is here. Don't move."

"Don't worry about that."

I let him be and walked down to the front. I intended to check behind the screen, but the entire back wall, painted a reflective light gray, made up the screen with no place to hide behind. I moved to the center and looked up toward Bozeman, scanning each of the dark leather seats as I did. I saw no one other than my musical partner.

Just beneath the projectionist's booth, I spotted a popcorn cart against the wall. I breathed deep, and either picked up or imagined the scent of fresh popped popcorn with an artificial buttery topping and an unhealthy portion of salt. Next to the cart was a portable bar, a duplicate of the one currently in service in the ballroom. I took a couple of steps to my right and enjoyed the deep pile carpet under my feet. Based on the luxurious feel of the place, I knew wouldn't find a single dropped kernel or soda-sticky spot in this theater, and I suspected no seats had wads of chewed gum beneath them. I trudged up the steps and whacked Bozeman's boots as I passed him.

"Wake up, big fella, let's go."

Together, we left the theater. I sighed and let my shoulders drop. I'd hoped to find Amelia and Jackie, or at least one of them, but I'd failed in my quest.

"Where to next?" Bozeman asked.

"Back in the ballroom, I guess. We can ask Brantley if he has the key to the other door," I answered.

Bozeman cocked a thumb at the last room as we stepped past. "What's in there?"

I looked toward the door that stood ajar. "Just a storeroom."

"Did you check in there?"

"Yeah, twice. No one's in there."

"Can we take another look? Just to be thorough?"

I shrugged. "Why not? After you."

Bozeman swung open the door and turned on the light. He entered, and I followed. While he stepped in to examine the first set of shelves, I leaned against the clinically white wall, a mistake I found, since the light switch jabbed into my back. I moved over an inch and removed the irritant. I followed Bozeman with my eyes as he made a slow loop around the room. He even stopped at the same large teacart and checked the interior, just like I had done.

"Satisfied?" I asked.

"Sure. What was behind the other door?"

I looked at Bozeman like he had an aardvark on his head. "What other door?"

"Come with me."

I followed Bozeman to the far wall, to the shelves with the

napkins. "Here."

"Here where?"

Bozeman crouched low and pointed at a set of scratches on the tile. As he moved his finger, I finally caught sight of the faint arc that opened into the room.

"Son of a gun. I missed that. How did you find it?" I asked.

"Dropped a napkin and picked it up. Spotted it then."

"I didn't see it. How does it open?" I asked.

Bozeman stood straight. "Well, I figure if it arcs out that way, the hinge is on the left side somewhere."

He grabbed the middle of the five shelves on the right side and pulled. Bozeman grunted, but other than that, nothing happened. He reached for the shelf above, then the shelf below, tugged with all his might, and again, nothing moved.

"Are you sure about there being a door here? Perhaps there was something else in the room, like a crate or something, and it scratched the floor?" I asked.

Bozeman crouched again, then got down on his hands and knees. He leaned over so his ear almost touched the floor. From his prone position, Bozeman reached out and touched the scratch with his fingertips, then traced it all the way to the shelving unit's feet.

"You're right. This doesn't match up completely. The scratches start about three inches from the feet, so whatever made these was out this way, and not flush with the shelves. Unless…"

I watched as Bozeman fondled the tiles around the unit's gray rubber feet. After he did it a first time, he did it a second.

"Bozeman? What are you doing?" I asked.

"Hold on a sec."

Bozeman got up and crawled on his hands and knees to the feet on the opposite side, went back to his belly, and ran his fingers along the surface of the tile. He stopped, got to his feet, and returned to the other side of the shelving unit.

"I think this unit moves out toward the center of the room

and then slides open," he said.

"How can that be? You tried moving it and it didn't budge."

"There must be a switch or latch or something to open it."

I smiled. "Again, just like in the movies?"

Bozeman grunted at me like an unhappy gorilla. "Just look for something, will you? Along the inside edges of the shelves. Probably close to the wall."

"Okay, okay."

I headed to the side of the shelving unit and wrapped my hand around the front vertical support. I ran my hand from shelf to shelf, and besides the cool stainless steel, I sensed nothing else. Moving on, I did the same with the next support, and the next, and found nothing. In frustration, I sighed and gave up on trying to find the secret by touch. Instead, I selected the third shelf to start with, and removed all the napkins from my half of the shelf and leaned over and pushed my way in until I felt my head touch the back wall.

From there, I visually inspected not only the vertical supports but also the horizontal ones on the shelf above and below me. I spotted nothing, so I slithered out from the shelves and repeated the process with the shelf above. No longer worried about keeping the creases neat, I threw the napkins aside, then used the bottom shelf to boost myself up to the fourth. I checked the vertical supports first, failed, then looked at the shelf above me. There I saw a small button, no larger than a pea.

"I think I got it," I said.

I pushed the button and waited breathlessly.

Inside the wall, I picked up the sound of a light click. I pushed away from the wall and felt the shelf move with me.

"Whoa, hold on," Bozeman said behind me.

Bozeman held the shelves while I freed myself from its clutches. I stepped backward until I contacted the teacart and told Bozeman to go ahead. He pulled the middle shelf and the entire unit moved forward a few inches. He grabbed the right side, pulled, and we both watched as the unit came away from the wall. I had wrongly assumed that the shelves backed up against the wall, but it turned out that a portion of the wall was connected to the shelves. When Bozeman pulled it open, he revealed a wooden door.

"Think it's locked?" I asked.

"I hope not. There's no keyhole. Let's give it a pull."

I stepped up, wrapped my hand around the knob, and gave it a yank. I expected a bunch of resistance that wasn't there, so the door flew open. The tiny room contained no light source of its own, but the storeroom provided all the light I needed.

At last, we'd found Jackie and Amelia.

CHAPTER NINETEEN

One would think the sight of two women bound and gagged would leave me stunned and frightened, but instead a sense of relief fell over me like a warm sunrise on a winter's morning. Someone had trussed the women up like calves at the local rodeo, except instead of rope, they were bound by black duct tape around their ankles and wrists. A short length of tape wrapped around their heads prevented them from speaking, not that they would, since they were both unconscious.

"Are they alive?" Bozeman asked.

The women laid sprawled on the floor facing each other. I saw Amelia's chest rise and fall like she'd just run a mile, and after a second, Jackie took a breath as well. "Yes, but I think Amelia is having trouble. Help me get them out of here."

I moved farther into the room, careful not to step on anyone, and bent over to lift Amelia's shoulders while Bozeman stepped in and attended to her feet.

"Let me know when you're ready," he said when he got into position.

"Okay, go," I said. I grunted, lifted Amelia an inch, then

dropped her. "Sorry about that."

"You want to switch positions?" Bozeman asked.

"Not necessary. I lost my grip. Let's go again."

I counted to three this time, and since that magical spell always worked, I managed to lift Amelia's torso and together, Bozeman and I shuffled her out into the more spacious storeroom.

Bozeman searched for the edge of tape around Amelia's legs but didn't find it. "You have anything sharp on you?"

"Usually only my wit," I responded as I dug around in my pocket for Brantley's keys. My hand closed around them, and I tossed them to Bozeman. "Try these."

While Bozeman tried to free Amelia's legs, I worked at the tape covering her mouth. Someone had wrapped it around her head three times, so it extended from just below her nose to just above her chin. With a delicate touch, I started with her face. I pushed on her cheek to give me some slack and got a fingernail under the tape's edge. I lifted it and followed it around her head until I found where it had ripped from the roll near her left ear.

"Give me a hand here, Boze," I said.

Bozeman set the keys down and joined me.

"Sit her up," I said.

Bozeman grabbed Amelia's shoulders and gently got her to a sitting position. Once she was up, I at last loosened the tape edge and began to unwrap her. With the speed of a running sloth, I peeled the tape away, careful to take as little skin and hair with it as I could. On the second loop around her head, I discovered her abductor had covered her mouth with a dark red napkin. After I completed the third loop, I tossed the tape to the side and removed the napkin that had not only covered her mouth but was half in it as well.

As Bozeman watched, I gently removed the napkin from Amelia's throat. She took in a large gasp of air, and then her breathing returned to normal.

"Lay her down," I said.

Bozeman did and made a move to free her feet when I stopped him.

"Hold off on that. Let's go get Jackie first," I said.

He nodded, and we returned to the little room where we found Jackie still sleeping. This time, I let Bozeman take her top half, and together we wrestled her from the tiny spot and into the main room. I repeated the process to remove the tape from around her mouth and found she had a dark blue napkin shoved into her throat. Once I removed the obstruction from her mouth, Bozeman returned to undo Amelia's bindings as I worked on Jackie's.

I glanced over and saw Bozeman was still sawing away at Amelia's tape with the keys, and I guessed maybe that wasn't the best way to go about it. I ran a fingernail around Jackie's taped legs until I found the edge, picked at it until I got enough to grip, and pulled at it. The satisfying sound of the tape releasing filled my ears as I pulled, and after a half dozen loops around Jackie's legs, I released the last of the tape and placed it on the floor.

"Do you think they're going to want fingerprints from that?" Bozeman asked.

"I don't know," I said. "Nor do I really care at this point."

After I freed Jackie's legs, I started to work on her bound wrists. Fortunately, her assailant had ducted taped them together in front of her, so I didn't need to roll her over. I repeated the method I used on her legs, and soon I had her arms free and resting at her sides.

"Jackie?" I yelled. "Can you hear me? Jackie?"

I received no response at all, so I shook her shoulders.

"Jackie? Hey! Are you there? Hello?"

I still got no response. Whatever they had drugged her with was effective. As a last resort, I picked up her left arm and cradled it in my lap. I took her hand and pinched the tip of her index finger as hard as I dared. Finally, I got a response from her as she moaned and instinctively pulled her hand away.

"What are they on?" Bozeman asked.

I shook my head. "No clue, but it has to be something powerful. I can't bring her around at all. How are you doing over there?"

I glanced over, and saw Bozeman had Amelia's tape removed, and he had no better luck at reviving her than I did Jackie.

"Should we splash some water on them?" Bozeman asked.

I considered it for a moment. "No. Then they'd be unconscious and wet. I think the best we can do here is let them sleep it off until they either come to themselves, or we can get them some proper medical attention."

"So now what?"

"I'll be back in a jiffy." I rose and left Jackie lying by herself on the floor. With haste, I returned to the secret room and looked around, even though there wasn't much to see.

The room itself was only four feet square. Its spartan walls were unfinished, and whoever had created the room hadn't even bothered with drywall. The prominent feature was the vertical wooden studs that went from floor to ceiling every sixteen inches. Besides the studs, I saw cables in various colors, mostly in white and black. In the far corner, a small-diameter copper pipe came out of the wall, did a ninety-degree turn, and disappeared into the unfinished wood floor.

I crouched low to look for clues, but spotted nothing. No telltale torn buttons, no hair samples, no wayward threads, no confession notes. Nothing but dust, so far as I could tell. Dejected, I left the little room and rejoined Bozeman.

"Find anything?" he asked when I joined him.

"Not a thing. I couldn't even guess what that room is supposed to be used for."

"What's in there?"

"Conduit mostly, and I think a gas pipe."

Bozeman shrugged. "Now what?"

I shook my head, trying to produce a plan out of thin air. After all, I didn't have many items remaining on my list of things to do. I'd found the missing keys, and the missing women. All I needed to do was figure out the last missing piece of who the culprit was. Oh, and find the missing gun.

"Well, I'd really like to figure out who caused this entire mess and pass the baton back to Viola. And I'd love a nap and a shower. And maybe a peanut butter and jelly sandwich."

Bozeman chuckled. "I know what you mean. I've run out of gas and patience for this night. And I like your idea about the sandwich."

I sighed out of weariness more than anything. "We'll have to get Laurel to make them for us when we get back to the bus."

Bozeman got up, stretched, and took a seat on top of the large teacart. "There's something I don't understand."

"Just one?" I teased.

"Exactly one. How is it that of the three of us, Laurel makes the best sandwiches? I mean, it's the same ingredients, same counter, same knife, same everything. Yet somehow, they're on another level than what either of us make."

I hadn't thought about it, but now the question pushed into my already crowded head. He was correct. Laurel's sandwiches were far superior to the ones Bozeman or I made. It must have had something to do with the peanut butter to jelly ratio she used.

I got poised to offer my opinion when I got interrupted.

"Codi?" My name was but a whisper, but it shot right into my ears and caught my attention as easily as a firework exploding in the sky.

I looked down and saw Jackie's bright blue eyes staring at me.

"Hey, you," I answered. I found Jackie's hand and gave it a squeeze. "How are you feeling?"

She blinked a couple of times. "Tired. My head hurts. What

happened?"

"I'm hoping you can tell me. Do know where you are? Or remember how you got here?"

Jackie closed her eyes. I waited, and after half a minute I thought she'd gone back to sleep. Then she opened them. They seemed a bit more alert than a minute before.

"I was in the ballroom. I felt a pinch on my shoulder, then I overheard some voices, then I think I fell asleep."

"Which shoulder? And whose voice was it?"

"Left. It really hurt."

I looked at her left shoulder and spotted a small dot of red. I lifted the fabric of her sleeve and looked closer. There on her arm right above a freckle was the spot where someone had injected her with something.

"Hey, Bozeman, can you come down here and see if Amelia's got any needle marks on her?"

Bozeman did as I asked while I returned Jackie's dress to normal.

"Someone has drugged you with something. Do you understand?"

Jackie's eyes never left mine, and she blinked a few times before my words finally sunk into her head and she nodded.

"Do you remember the voice? Who did you hear?"

"I'm thirsty. Can I have something to drink?" Jackie asked.

"Bozeman, can you get her some water?" I asked, without breaking eye contact.

"Hold on, let me finish this first."

I waited, unaware I'd been holding my breath until my lungs started to burn. I exhaled and drew in a fresh breath.

"Found it, Codi. There's a blood spot on her right thigh. I'll assume that's where she got hit, because that's the only mark I found. Stay here and I'll go get that water."

I looked up and watched as Bozeman selected a glass from a shelf and headed for the bathroom. I returned my attention to

Jackie. She'd closed her eyes again.

"Jackie? You with me?"

"Yes."

"Who did you hear?"

"Here." The words I heard got combined with the glass that floated into my visual field.

"Bozeman has water for you. Let's sit you up."

I struggled to lift Jackie's shoulders, but eventually got her to a sitting position. I repositioned myself so I kneeled behind her, and I wrapped my arms around her.

"Jackie. Have some water."

Jackie shook her head twice, like she'd just walked face first into a spiderweb. Bozeman held the glass steady to her lips, and when the water touched them, Jackie slowly raised her arm and took the glass from him. She drank deeply and finished three quarters of the water before I had a chance to tell her to take it easy. Jackie smiled and passed the glass back to Bozeman.

She found words, and they came out stronger than before. "Thank you. I needed that."

"Jackie, please. Can you tell us who did this to you?"

Jackie took a deep breath, exhaled, and finally gave me the answer I'd been waiting for.

"Brantley. He did it."

"You're sure?" I asked.

"One hundred percent. He did this to me, and I'm sure he's behind everything else that's happened tonight."

"Brantley? But why?"

Jackie shrugged. "That would be a question for him, wouldn't it?"

She was correct. "I guess I'll need to go ask him. Would you do me a favor and stay here and watch over Amelia?"

"I will," Jackie said.

I let her go and clambered to my feet. "Bozeman, would you care to join me?"

He didn't answer but based on his clenched fists and the look in his eye, he didn't need to.

From the storeroom, we hustled directly to the ballroom. Bozeman had stepped in front of me, and I struggled to keep up with him. Even moving into a light jog, I could barely match his lengthy gait. He stopped briefly just inside the ballroom door, and since I hadn't expected it, I almost ran right into his back. Bozeman paused for just a moment, spotted Brantley across the room, deep in conversation with Claude, and resumed his journey.

"Bozeman!" I shouted, trying to get him to stop, but he didn't. I'd seen Bozeman in a rage before, and although he wasn't anywhere near his worst, I still couldn't stop him.

Everyone in the room reacted to my yell, and every head turned in our direction. Brantley turned just in time for Bozeman to get close enough to grab him by the shoulders and bend him backwards over the table Brantley stood next to.

Without a word, Bozeman made a fist and drew his arm back, and I knew if I didn't do something quick, Bozeman would end up on the wrong end of a murder charge. Especially with the police chief watching.

I took the only action I could. I jumped and grabbed Bozeman's right arm. Normally, he'd have no problems lifting me, even with a single arm, but since he didn't realize I was there, I threw him off balance with my weight. He stumbled backward, tripped over the leg of a chair, and fell. Since I was still dangling from his arm like a Christmas ornament, I hit the deck as well. Lucky for me, I didn't get his full weight on top of me. Instead, I only received his elbow in my gut. I lost my breath, then heaved when I couldn't catch it back. I felt like his one blow had snapped several ribs, ruptured my spleen, and destroyed my soul.

Bozeman rolled over onto his side, and when he did, I sat up. I managed a couple of deep breaths, deduced I wasn't dead, and got to my feet. By the time I returned to Brantley, Claude had peeled him off the table like the sticker from a banana.

It was my turn, and I got toe to toe with Brantley and shoved my finger at his chest.

"You tried to kill me!" I screamed in his face.

Brantley raised his hands to protect his face. "I didn't do anything."

Claude stepped in front of me and forced me to back up a few feet. He put a hand lightly on my shoulder to restrain me. "What's going on here?" he asked.

"Brantley murdered Hawthorne, assaulted Viola, and shot at me," I said.

My comment drew some interest, and the circle of people around us grew. Helen, Loren, Laurel, and Viola had joined the party.

Bozeman hadn't found his feet yet, so Loren stepped next to me and wrapped his paw around Claude's wrist.

"You should let her be," Loren whispered.

Claude hesitated for a moment, then dropped his arm. "I only want to know what's going on."

"Boze and I found Jackie and Amelia in a secret room. He drugged and bound them up with duct tape. When Jackie came to, she told us that Brantley drugged her. It's not a far leap from kidnapping to think he did the murder as well."

"This all true, Brantley?" Viola asked.

"Of course not. Only pure speculation on her part."

"You had all the access, Brantley," I said. "And you had the keys to enter the locked areas, and you had the app. You controlled the gong and the lights when Hawthorne got shot. And the lights when you struck Viola. I'll bet your fingerprints are all over the note you left me, and the candlestick that struck Viola."

In a feeble attempt to regain his composure, Brantley took a moment to smooth out his tunic. I noticed the hole in his tights had expanded and ran all the way up his thigh.

"It's all circumstantial," he argued. "Should I remind you that you found no gun on me? Or that I stood almost right next to you when you got shot at? Or that it was Amelia with the app on her phone? Did you even see me with a phone tonight? No, you didn't. Because I don't have it with me, because I follow the rules."

"Is that it?" I prodded. "Did you get tired of following the rules? Sick of being underpaid and taken advantage of? Did you want a bigger piece of the pie?"

Brantley shook his head. "You have no clue what you're talking about. You've got nothing on me. No motive, no opportunity, no evidence."

"You mean no evidence except for Jackie's eyewitness account," I said.

"Don't forget about Amelia's," Bozeman added as he stepped to my side.

Brantley opened his mouth, but only a single unrecognizable syllable slipped out before he shut it again.

Viola put something cold in my hands. I looked down and saw her handcuffs.

"Do the honors, Codi," she said.

I lifted the cuffs and dangled them in front of Brantley's face. "Bozeman, Loren, could y'all help me get him turned around?"

Before the men could move, a gunshot rang out. As one, we turned around and faced the direction of the ballroom door. There, Amy Ewing had a gun pointed at the group. The muzzle smoked, and my eyes went to the ceiling, where I spotted a hole in the plaster above her.

"I told you she'd figure it out somehow. Come on. Let's go. No one else move."

Brantley pushed his way through the crowd and strode to Amy's side. He leaned toward her and she took her eyes off of us long enough to give him a kiss. When they finished, Amy raised the gun and shot another round into the ceiling. Almost everyone in the group instinctively ducked, and during the distraction, Amy and Brantley disappeared from the ballroom.

CHAPTER TWENTY

I looked at Bozeman, and he gave me a single nod before taking off at a dead-on sprint. Although I started my run only a second behind him, he disappeared out the door before I'd taken only three steps. Laurel chased me out the door, and someone followed her, but in the excitement, I couldn't tell who it was.

"Bozeman, wait up!" I screamed as I ran as fast as my short legs would carry me. Once I left the ballroom, I noticed he'd slowed to a walk, and when he got to the junction of the corridor, he stopped in his tracks. I got near and was about to pass him when he grabbed my shoulder and moved me back behind him.

"Whoa, there filly," he said as he slammed me into the wall. "Sorry about that."

I wanted to submit a protest when I overheard a report, and a bullet struck the wall to my left. Had I gone out into the hallway, I would have caught that round right in the chest.

"Thanks," I whispered.

"No problem," Bozeman said. "Now stay there a second."

I had no trouble complying with his order. As I stayed flat against the wall, Bozeman peeked around the corner. His head snapped back, and another bullet came whizzing by.

"I don't think she likes you," I said.

"There's hope for us yet. Don't give up."

I sensed someone brush against my left shoulder, and a turn of my head confirmed Laurel had arrived. Loren was right next to her.

"Hey," she said.

"Hey yourself. Loren, I don't suppose that armor you're wearing is bulletproof?" I asked.

He shook his head. "Nope, sorry."

I shrugged and turned my attention back to Bozeman. I wanted to ask what plan he had in mind, but before I could speak, he took off in a full run once again. Slowly, I moved up and looked around the corner. I saw the door at the far end of the hall closing, and Bozeman was in a full sprint to catch it before it locked. He arrived in the nick of time, and I saw him reach out and grab the knob just before the door slammed closed.

He started to struggle when someone on the other side attempted to pull the door closed. Bozeman took the knob in both hands and leaned back. "I could use some help here," he called out.

Loren answered the call and ran down the hallway. He wrapped his arms around Bozeman's waist and pulled. He must have caught him tight because Bozeman began to hiss like a balloon losing air.

"This isn't going to work. I'm losing my grip," Bozeman shouted.

I took that as my clue to jump in. After a quick assessment of the situation, I ran to Loren, but rather than give him a bear hug, I unsheathed Excalibur, turned it around, and shoved the hilt into the door. I let go of the blade just as Bozeman's hands slipped off the knob. Since Loren was still tugging on him, he and Bozeman toppled like dominoes. The door banged against the hilt, and I saw someone trying to push it away. On impulse, I kicked the tip forward, then stood on the blade. The person on the other end of the hilt tried to pull the sword toward them instead of pushing it out, but the sword's guard caught against the jamb and effectively locked it in place. We were in a stalemate, and I felt the sword go slack, so I assumed they had given up.

I put my ear to the door and listened. "I think they left," I said.

Loren scolded me. "Come away from there before you get your ear pierced by a bullet."

Undaunted, I swung the door open and looked. The room beyond was empty, so I threw the door open wide and stepped inside with Loren, Bozeman, and Laurel right on my heels. The room looked like a large parlor dominated by a wide, winding staircase. Opposite from where I stood was another door, this one ajar.

"Now what?" Bozeman asked.

"Now we break into groups. You and Loren take the room across from here, Laurel and I will check upstairs."

Bozeman frowned at me. "You sure that's a good idea? Me or Loren could come with you."

"Oh, please. Just go. The bad guys are getting away."

Loren wanted to protest, but I cut that off by pointing in the direction I wanted them to go. After a moment, they took the hint and rushed across the room.

"You ready to save the day?" I asked.

Laurel nodded. Together, we approached the stairs and started our climb. At the top, we found two closed doors at the top, and we each took one.

"This one is locked," Laurel said.

This was supposed to be someone's house, so I couldn't imagine why someone would have so many locked doors. I figured Hawthorne either had too many secrets or not enough trust.

"This one isn't," I said when I pushed the large double doors open. I suspected that this way would lead to the bedrooms, and when I ducked into the first room I saw, I realized I was right. The room contained a queen-sized poster bed, a chest of drawers, and a matching nightstand. A coat tree stood sentry in one corner, and that was it for furniture.

"Must be a guest room," Laurel said.

"Check under the bed. I'll check out the closet," I said.

I moved across the room with purpose, not wanting to dally, and opened what I assumed was the closet door. It turned out to be a short hallway with doors on either side. To the left I found an empty walk-in closet, to the right I found an equally empty bathroom.

"No one here," I said as I passed Laurel and moved on to the next room. The next three rooms were exactly the same as the first, right down to the bedspreads. In the fifth room, we struck pay dirt. The room looked like a pack of wild dingoes had come through.

The bed was the same, a queen-sized poster bed, but instead of a clean, white bedspread, this bed contained one in a soft pink. Only a corner of the bed was empty and based on the found pairs of shoes scattered on the floor, I got the impression that's where the owner changed her shoes. The rest of the bed had piles of clutter with all kinds of things, mostly clothing. In one look, I spotted several shirts, three pairs of jeans, two discarded dresses, and a pink sweatshirt with a picture of a unicorn giving me the finger.

I moved to the drawers. Again, they were the same as the others we'd seen, but this one the owner had topped with bottles of perfumes, body lotions, creams, and things I didn't recognize. Overcome by the combinations of so many flowery odors, I coughed and stepped away.

"Whose room is this?" Laurel asked as she stood after looking under the bed. "There's no room under there for anything but a dust bunny. Books, unpaired shoes, a couple of shirts, and a couple of small boxes."

"It's Jackie's room," I said.

"How can you tell?"

I pointed toward the dresser. The only organized thing in the room was the autographed shirt I'd given her, hung neatly on a hanger, the hanger clinging to the knob of the top drawer.

"Anyone in the closet or bathroom?" I asked.

Laurel disappeared for a moment, then returned with the report. "I've never seen a closet so full. It's stuffed with clothing and other things. The bathroom is a mix of beauty supplies and used towels all over the floor."

"Let's go then," I said.

The next room we entered belonged to Hawthorne. I stopped the second I entered the room to take it all in. The room looked at least three times the size of the other bedrooms we'd explored. The centerpiece was a massive king-sized canopy bed, complete with the curtains I'd always associated with Ebenezer Scrooge in the movies. Unlike Jackie's, someone had made his bed with military precision, and his deep brown bedspread had not a crease to be seen. I walked across the deep pile carpet to the bed, which came up to just above my hip. If I wanted a nap, I'd need a ladder to get in.

I dropped to the floor and looked under the bed and spotted nothing at all, not even a random piece of fuzz. I stood and visually inspected the remainder of the room. He had two dressers and a nightstand on each side of the bed, both holding ornate table lamps. One wall held three bookcases, although only one held books. The other contained knick-knacks and photographs framed in silver.

"I'll check the closet and bathroom," Laurel said.

While she explored the interior of the suite, I leaned against the bed and stared at the bookcases. Something wasn't quite right about them, but I couldn't put a finger on what.

Laurel reappeared. "Nothing in the closet except a thousand suits and two thousand pairs of shoes, all in boxes, I might add. I don't think he owned a pair of jeans."

"What about the bathroom?" I asked.

"We could live in there. Walk-in rain shower, Jacuzzi tub. There's even a fridge in there. Seriously, Codi, who has a fridge in the bathroom?"

"Rich people," I answered without thinking. "You notice anything off about those bookcases?"

Laurel joined me against the bed and stared at them for a minute.

"Other than the picture on the floor, no."

My eyes passed from the bookcase to the floor and noticed the picture sitting on the carpet. It was a small one, like a photograph you'd get out of a photo booth at a county fair. Even with the ornate silver frame, it had almost disappeared into the deep carpet. I retrieved it, then tried to figure out where it called home. At last, I decided on a spot and set it on the shelf. Once I placed it back, I began to run my fingers on the bookcase sides and beneath the shelves.

"What are you doing?" Laurel asked.

"Searching for this." I pushed a button, heard a familiar click, then pulled out the bookcase. It swung open and I spotted another door. I expected it to be locked tight, but it opened right away. There, on the safe room bunk, sat a startled Brantley.

When I opened the door, Brantley jumped to his feet like a jittery deer, slammed me into the safe room door, and ran. I thought Laurel was going to let him pass, but just as he got to her, she shot out a foot and tripped him. He hit her foot, took another two awkward strides forward, then fell. I heard a sickening thud when his head hit a dresser, and he was still.

To make sure he wasn't faking, I moved to him and assessed his condition. He was down for the count. With Laurel's help, I got Viola's handcuffs around his wrists. To me, the sound of the handcuffs tightening was the most satisfying thing I'd heard all night.

"Now what?" Laurel asked.

"We have to wait for the boys to find us, or for him to wake up. I'm in no mood to carry him."

"Screw that. I'm sick of waiting. I've been waiting all night."

Laurel left my side and returned a minute later with a liter-sized bottle of water. "Want a drink?"

I nodded, took the bottle, and drank. The cold water felt refreshing, and I didn't realize how thirsty I was. I handed the bottle back to Laurel, who also drank.

"You want more?" she asked.

I shook my head. I thought she intended to cap the bottle and save the rest for later, but instead she inverted the bottle and dumped the rest of the contents on Brantley's head.

Brantley came too in a flash. He sputtered, realized where he was, and tried to escape. I put a foot on him and held him down.

"Now where are you trying to run off to?"

With Laurel's help, I got Brantley to his feet, and together we escorted him back to the ballroom. To my surprise, we received a round of applause as we entered, our prey out in front of us, doing his own personal walk of shame. I spotted Loren and Bozeman, then saw Amy tied to a chair. We moved Brantley over to Amy and plopped him down next to her.

"Everything go okay?" I asked.

Bozeman nodded. "Just fine. Caught up to her in Hawthorne's office. All we had to do was wait until she ran out of bullets, then we went in and got her."

After I gave him a hug, I moved away from the gathered crowd. I stepped back to the stage, my sanctuary. I took a seat on the riser and leaned my back against Bozeman's amplifier. After a few cleansing breaths, I closed my eyes, ready to rest.

*

Two days later, Laurel, Bozeman, and I stepped off the bus and headed into Loren's diner. The hostess greeted us and led us directly to Loren's booth. I grinned when I got there, and Viola stood up and gave me a big hug.

"How are you feeling?" I asked once she released me from her clutches.

"Sit down. I'm good. I spent a night in the hospital for observation and had to undergo a few scans and a day of boredom, but I'm good now. Codi, I have to give you credit. You did a great job. Your dad would be proud of the way you handled yourself under such extreme circumstances."

I slid into the booth, followed by Laurel. Bozeman took a seat on Loren's bench. I wasn't sure how to move forward with the small talk, but I got saved when Loren appeared from the kitchen, carrying a large plate. He set it on the table and my mouth drooled the second I saw the steaming cinnamon rolls with the white frosting dripping down the side. The smell of the cinnamon took me back to helping my grandma in her kitchen.

Loren grinned and sat down next to Bozeman. He took a moment to serve a cinnamon roll to everyone at the table, passed out the forks, and ordered us to dig in.

"So, Viola, give us the scoop," I said as I dug into my roll. I cut off a bite and put it into my mouth, where it practically melted with one flavor after another.

Viola threw me a cross look and chided me. "You know I can't talk about an ongoing investigation."

I dropped my eyes to my breakfast and silently cut off another chunk.

"If I did," Viola started. "I'd tell you it was Amy, not Brantley controlling the lights and the gong using his phone."

"Then Brantley shot Hawthorne," Laurel said.

Viola nodded. "He also whacked me with the candlestick in the ballroom."

"And the shot at me?" I asked.

"That was Amy," Viola said. "Good thing, too. I think had it been Brantley, you wouldn't be here today getting frosting on your chin."

I hoped she was kidding, but when I touched my chin, my fingers came away with a dollop of sugary goodness on them.

"How did we manage to get trapped in there all night?" Bozeman asked.

"That was Brantley too. When my people went through the ballroom, we found a blocker he activated to block any phone calls from getting in or out. He also called off security, too, which is why no one came to our rescue."

"Did you find out how Jackie and Amelia are doing?" I asked.

Viola finished the bite in her mouth and washed it down with some orange juice before she answered. "They will both be fine. Like me, they stayed in the hospital for a few hours until the doctors discovered what Brantley and Amy drugged them with. They got released about the same time, and even shared a cab ride home."

"That part I don't get. Why abduct the women?" I asked.

Viola sighed. "Brantley and Amy thought it would deflect attention away from them. It would have been easy to say they slipped out of the house, and no one would have been the wiser."

"You know anything about the business? Is Loren going to lose this place?" Bozeman asked.

Loren gave us a grin wide enough to count every bright, white tooth in his mouth. "Nope. I'm good. Hawthorne was the only person in town with enough capital to carry the project forward. I heard this morning the entire deal is off."

"I guess I'll have to wait a little longer to get my bigger office in a nice new building," Viola said. "But that's okay with me. It turns out Hawthorne had a bigger heart than anyone realized. According to Claude, the estate and all the personal property will get sold off, and the proceeds divided up among the many local charities in town."

"What about the businesses?" I asked.

Voila laughed. She wiped her mouth and set her napkin on the table. "You'll never believe this one. Claude told me Hawthorne's heir apparent will run the businesses."

"I didn't know he had one," Loren said.

"He does, and you met her. Helen Troy."

Based on the gasps, Viola's words shocked everyone at the table, except Loren.

"What?" I asked. "How did that happen?"

"Yep, it turns out that Helen is Hawthorne's half-sister."

"She wasn't just hanging around the office giving Hawthorne personal training services," I said.

"Nope. Turns out he was looking to retire soon, and they were using her ruse as a cover story, so no one would be the wiser."

"One last thing I need to know," I said. "Why? Why did Brantley and Amy do it?"

Viola drained her glass before she answered. "Well, it turns out that Brantley was the wiser and knew that Hawthorne wanted to step down. From what he gathered, Helen wasn't as fond of rebuilding the entire town as Hawthorne was and wanted to scale way back. She also wasn't fond of Brantley, so he knew he'd be out the door soon. So, he thought if he could get rid of them both, he could somehow control his own fate."

"Okay," I said. "That explains Brantley. What about Amy?"

"That one comes down to a combination of convenience and greed. She wanted to escape Danny's problem with the bottle, and she'd also invested heavily in several of the companies that would benefit from the construction projects. From what my investigators have revealed so far, she positioned herself to make millions. She saw Brantley as a way to get out of her marriage and into the life of a millionaire. Turns out the end result is bad for both of them."

I finished the last of the cinnamon roll and licked the fork clean of frosting. "That was delicious, Loren. Thank you."

"No. Thank you, Codi. And Bozeman and Laurel as well. We don't know what would have gone down had you not been there. And trust me, you've got another batch of rolls and a couple of pies going with you when you leave here."

I patted my stomach. "Sounds good to me."

"Speaking of leaving, where are you headed next?" Viola asked.

I shrugged. I had the destination written on a calendar on the bus, but I hadn't looked at it in a bit. The location didn't matter. I knew there would be music and adventure regardless of where the bus took us.

ABOUT THE AUTHOR

Dan DeKoning was born and raised in Milwaukee, Wisconsin, and currently lives in Knoxville, Tennessee with his wife and their cats.

He is a storyteller and poet who loves to write in a variety of genres and themes. He is also a voracious reader who loves to read anything he can get his hands on.

When he's not writing, you can find him hunting for treasures in used bookstores, or out exploring the planet, or geocaching, or searching for adventures and stories to tell.

ALSO BY DAN DEKONING

This is Dan DeKoning's complete library at the time of publication, but Dan has new books coming out all the time. Sign up for his newsletter at DanDeKoning.com to stay up to date on new releases.

Fiction
Déjà Vu
The Haunting of Hyacinth House
How Deep the Darkness

Geocaching Mystery Series
The Cacheland Conspiracy
The Quincy Bay Quandary
The Secret of the Seven Valleys
The Geocaching Mystery Omnibus – Volume 1

Codi Cassidy Cozy Mystery Series
Acoustics and Alibis
Ballads and Bloodshed
Codas and Calibers
Codi Cassidy Cozy Omnibus – Volume 1

Poetry Collections
Lost and Found
Random Thoughts

www.ingramcontent.com/pod-product-compliance
Lightning Source LLC
Chambersburg PA
CBHW061527310726
48972CB00008B/2346